CHANGES

*In a
Little Gay Bar*

by
Nick DiMartino

University Book Store Press
Seattle, Washington

CHANGES
Copyright © 2006 by Nick DiMartino
Anna Micklin, publishing coordinator
Jake Monderen, photography and cover design
Brad Herst, technical consultant

UNIVERSITY BOOK STORE PRESS
Espresso Book Machine
First Printing: September 2012

This is entirely a work of fiction. The characters are invented, and should not be confused with real people.

8 September 2005 – 16 April 2006
All rights reserved.

ISBN: 978-1-937358-18-1

UNIVERSITY BOOK STORE
4326 University Way NE
Seattle, Washington 98105
www.ubookstore.com
206-634-3400

For autographed copies, with free shipping, call:
206-543-5896

CHANGES
In a Little Gay Bar

1. Good for You — 5
2. Solo — 14
3. King of the Seas — 23
4. The Third Bathroom — 33
5. Fathers and Sons — 43
6. Jealous Boyfriend — 50
7. Force of Nature — 61
8. Kiss of the Pool Shark — 68
9. Peacemaker — 75
10. The Source of All Pain — 84
11. Divided Attention — 94
12. Logical Grounds for Hope — 101
13. We Don't Play Trivia — 108
14. Those Were the Days — 116
15. Double Header — 123
16. Boogeyman — 131
17. Lupe's Sister — 141
18. Queen of the Fairies — 148
19. Three Hundred Aspirin — 160
20. The Palm Reader — 168
21. Uncle Vai — 179
22. The Spoiler — 196
23. Bad Boys — 210
24. Not-So-Great Expectations — 219

GOOD FOR YOU

I thought our friendship would last a lifetime.

Instead it ended at exactly ten minutes to midnight. For some reason I glanced at my watch that Saturday in July when he stormed out of the tavern, leaving me stranded and friendless in my new life.

Maybe I should never have gone. I had been sound asleep that hot summer night when he called, so it must have been sometime after ten. Jordan knew he was waking me, but that's the privilege of your best friend, isn't it?

"I'm depressed," he said. "I need to go out. Get dressed. I'm coming over to get you."

"Wait," I qualified. "I'm not going to one of those bars you like, the ones where the music is so loud you can't hear yourself think."

"Sure, sure, wherever, I don't care," he said. "I just need some fresh air. I need a beer. I'll show you that little gay bar in Wallingford I keep telling you about."

Changes

He had certainly been telling me about the place. That's an understatement. He'd been drilling it into my head for weeks. He wouldn't let up on his new obsession, which was getting me to walk up to this little bar alone. It's two miles away, an easy walk, good exercise, sure.

Jordan's reasoning: I'll never know how to be myself as long as he's always there beside me.

I don't go out alone. I admit it. That's just not me. I only go out with a friend, usually my best friend, which means usually Jordan Perez. I panic at the thought of walking into a gay bar without someone else walking in front of me. Jordan attracts so much attention that going anywhere with him I get social interaction without very much risk, and sometimes I get his leftovers. Maybe some guys think if they get in good with me, they'll get Jordan. Or that we work as a team. Whatever. Who knows what other people think? Without Jordan, I'd have to walk into gay bars alone. And I don't do that.

"Okay, fine," I agreed. "I'll put in my contact lenses." Going to this little bar with Jordan for company would be much more comfortable than going there alone. "When are you coming over?"

"I'm leaving right now."

That could mean anything with Jordan, and it did. He lives fifteen minutes away. An hour later, his little car backed into a parking place at the foot of the stairs leading up to my house. I was on the porch waiting for him. As he came up the stairs two at a time, I noticed he was putting out a cigarette.

Changes

"You're smoking these days?"

He shrugged. "Eduardo smokes. We've been thinking about getting tattoos together."

"That'll be a trick. How are you going to keep his boyfriend from noticing?"

"Really small matching tattoos in a secret place."

As we walk down the stairs toward his car, his cell phone lets out its trill of warbling notes. He lunges for it, as if he's got five seconds before it detonates. Of course it's Eduardo, who has shaken his boyfriend off his trail and is going to be at Neighbors dancing tonight. He hopes Jordan can join him.

After murmuring far too many endearments in his most lovable voice, Jordan snaps off his cell phone and says, "Eduardo is on his way to Neighbors. He'll be waiting for us there."

I slide into the passenger seat and pull shut the door. "Why would Eduardo go to Neighbors, if you and I are going to Changes?"

Jordan starts the engine. "Because he wants to go dancing." He pulls out of the parking space. "He feels trapped and crowded. Dancing helps him center himself. I told him we'd meet him there."

I'm totally calm. "Let me out of this car right now," I say in my firm, no-nonsense voice. "Jordan, I'm not going to Neighbors and that's final. I refuse to be deafened and ignored and forced to watch you and Eduardo rub bodies together."

Changes

"We'll include you."

"Please. Our original plan. Only."

"Okay, okay, we'll stop by Changes first and see what it's like. It might be dead." Dead is Jordan's terminology for anything less than a bar packed with shirtless dancing bodybuilders on drugs.

"Great. Changes it is."

I didn't have any high expectations for this little experience. Who would bother wasting time in an out-of-the-way, dead-end tavern? It would probably turn out to be a graveyard for old gay dinosaurs and local weirdos. I would never have set foot there, except that Jordan wasn't the only one urging me to go there. Aaron, Jordan's lover and my therapist, had also quite separately been urging me to start going to bars alone. He'd also suggested Changes, with its not very threatening gay atmosphere. With both Jordan and Aaron urging me to do the same thing, I had to consider it.

Changes is within walking distance. Two miles isn't bad. I'm a walker. Of course, that's two miles each way, and it's uphill getting there, right at the time of night when I'd like to kick off my shoes and curl up in bed with a good book. Forcing myself to walk two miles at nine o'clock to face rejection alone in a gay bar won't be easy. But I can do it.

The tough part is doing it alone.

Jordan doesn't really understand. He thrives among the beauty sharks, in the body-bartering sector of the gay world, whereas I'm awkward and ill at ease, not to mention out of my

Changes

league. For our friendship to be healthy, I need to be an equal, and maybe I'll never learn how to do that as long as I keep acting like his sidekick.

It doesn't take long to drive out of the University District and across the freeway into Wallingford. The little bar is right on the main drag, but easy to miss because of its extremely low-key front – a bare wall with the name of the bar in metal letters over a black door.

Jordan flipped a U-turn right in the middle of 45th to slide into a parking spot on the corner. He snapped off the thundering sound system, and as usual, he threw me his inhaler to carry in my pocket in case he had an asthma attack. His own pants were too tight, the pockets too small. Then he trotted across the side street between two moving cars, and I ran after him.

He gave the black door a push and we stepped into the narrow, dimly-lit interior. I was surprised at how small it was. One long bar, and a pool table at the end of it, the whole place a little bigger than my apartment. A shelf of sports trophies, a line of pull-tab machines, and a wall of framed male nudes surrounded a handsome, thirty-foot red oak bar as a centerpiece.

"You want that new beer you like so much?" I ask him, as I step up to the bartender's station. "A Corona?" Corona is Jordan's new drink.

Eduardo drinks Corona.

Changes

Jordan nods. He's checking the place out. It's not his kind of bar. He'd call it dead. Good music, but not loud enough to rattle the walls. No pulsing house beat throbbing in the floor underfoot. Less than twenty guys. No one shirtless. No one dancing.

"And you?" says the bartender.

I realize he's talking to me. He's a good six feet tall, attractive and shaved bald, a broad-shouldered, butch hunk of a guy. I have no idea what I want. I reach into the blue for the name of a drink, any drink. "Long Island." To my surprise, the guy picks up four bottles at once and pours them simultaneously over ice cubes.

Jordan is checking out the pool table when I hand him his drink, and we drift down the bar toward the game in progress.

"This place will be good for you," he says.

"Spare me."

"You need to be forced out of your comfort zone."

"Comfort zone? I don't have one. I'm lonely, inhibited, and feel completely out of place. Does that sound comfortable to you?"

We've stopped in the middle of the bar, at a bottleneck where the coat rack, a row of coolers, and the end of the bar converge at the dart board. "I know you're going to hate me at first, but you need to be cut loose."

I hear condescension in his voice. "You're just tired of trying to help me find a boyfriend."

Changes

"You need to be forced to stand on your own two feet."

"That's easy to say while you're busy doing your little dance between Aaron and Eduardo."

A shout goes up from the pool table, startling both of us. Half a dozen young lesbians are cheering.

"You're refusing to see the situation. You need to build your confidence, and you can't do it around me. So that's why I have to use tough love."

"Is that what it's called? I'd call it getting rid of your pal, since all you want to do is screw your new boyfriend."

Guys are bumping around us and between us, trying to get through. We manage to work our way past the flying darts and pool cues, ending up on a bench on the other side of the pool table. Jordan can't take his eyes off the game. Eduardo plays pool.

"I can't believe you've never been to a bar alone."

"I thought bars were places you went with your buddies to meet sexy new people to date."

He sighs and shakes his head. "You're forcing me to cut you off."

That's enough. I've had it. I say, "Okay, okay, I don't agree, but fine, you win. I can go with the program. I'll do it. I'll stand on my own. Point taken. Checkmate. No more relying on you. I'll walk up to this little bar three times a week, minimum. End of story."

"Glad we got that settled. Okay, then, drink up. Let's head down to Neighbors and find our Chilean friend."

Changes

"Um, no thank you," I say decisively. "He's *your* Chilean friend."

"What now?"

"Go ahead. Eduardo is expecting you. I'll stay here and discover who I really am."

"Look, I'm too depressed to have to deal with you, too," he says. His eyes are flashing black and dangerous. He's pissed. "Do you have to be so dramatic about everything? Fine. Do what you want."

He storms out of Changes.

Jordan never goes anywhere without attracting attention, and he's certainly done it again. The big-chested, massive old stag with an apron looks up from his grill at me sympathetically as I go out the door. He thinks I've just had a lover's squabble with my high-maintenance boy-toy. He winks at me as I pass.

Jordan is standing outside the bar, arms folded across his chest, scowling, waiting for me.

"Listen, I'm asking you as my friend," he begins, standing in the middle of the sidewalk, blocking my way. "I'm depressed. I need someone along tonight. I don't want to be alone with Eduardo, not yet. I need to know that he still feels the same, that I'm the one he loves and not his boyfriend, because he's more sensitive than you realize, and blah blah blah," with more of the same. He can go on for days, rattling on about the new god in heaven. "Please, you can see how emotional I am. I'm asking you as a favor tonight."

Changes

"You've got a short memory," I say. "The last time you two started rubbing together on the dance floor, I had to take a taxi home."

"Just come to Neighbors. You'll have a good time."

"Neighbors is the one place in the world I'll *never* have a good time." Thundering music, flashing lights and strobes, a mob of shirtless show-offs bumping into each other on a packed dance floor where there's no use shouting because you can't be heard. Neighbors is for young beauties torturing each other with their bodies. It's not for me.

"So are you coming?" His voice is shaking.

I'm having a hard time talking. He's asking me a lot more than whether I want to go out with him tonight. "No."

"Well, I'm going."

"Okay. I can walk home."

"Great, then. See ya."

"See ya." I reach in my pocket and hand him his inhaler. He takes it. His hand briefly closes over mine.

Usually we hug. Not this time. Before I realize he's gone, Jordan is darting between a taxi and a bus, crossing the street toward his car. He squeals out of his parking space, off like a bullet by the shortest possible route to Eduardo.

I turn around and go back into Changes. My new life is just beginning. Next time I'm going to walk here alone.

Changes

SOLO

My best friend told me to do it.

My shrink told me to do it.

Finally one lonely night I grabbed my wallet, my summer windbreaker, and did it. I set out on a two-mile walk toward the little gay bar in the neighborhood next to mine.

And I walked there alone.

Why? The usual human reason. Something makes one person want to hold onto another. Once you've tasted physical pleasure, you crave it and hunt for it, and when you're gay you hunt for it harder. No one wants to walk the road alone. Unfortunately, I've made some bad choices in my life. A ticking clock is starting to thunder in my ears.

I couldn't rely on chance any longer. Why hadn't I found my soul mate yet? I wasn't searching aggressively enough, or at the right time, or in the right place. I'd begun to consider desperate measures, joining book clubs and potlucks and movie discussion groups.

So it's no surprise I settled for the same expedient compromise most of my community settles for – stalking the wild animals in bars. Where else would I find such a selection of attractive gay men whose thoughts were wandering toward physical pleasure?

Changes

Would they be safe? Would they be sane? Would I ever want to introduce them to my parents?

That was the gamble.

On that night in late July, as I closed and locked my front door and set out for Wallingford on my first solo adventure, I couldn't help but think, "Aaron would be proud of me." He was the reason I did it.

Aaron Weinstein wasn't my shrink anymore, but he'd been my shrink back when I needed one, the best shrink I could have asked for. After getting me back on my psychological feet he'd inadvertently become Jordan's lover in a sudden pairing that seemed too good to be true. Jordan Perez, my best friend for over a decade, had landed a smart, attractive man twenty years older who had buckets of charm, brains, the compassion that comes from facing tragedy, and a streetwise wisdom. Aaron Weinstein was an educated, athletic professional who adored him and could afford him. This was the man Jordan was deceiving. Given a choice, I would have begged not to know about it. Knowing more than I wanted to know, I had been avoiding Aaron.

So I wasn't exactly delighted when I ran into him at the Starbuck's down on Olive Way. By the time we recognized each other's voices and realized we were literally sitting with our backs to each other in the same coffee house, we were both so hyper-caffeinated that we cried as we hugged each other. I knew he was HIV-positive, and that it had progressed

Changes

into full-blown AIDS. He'd always been a perceptive guy, and his intimacy with mortality had made him almost clairvoyant with understanding. When he looked in my eyes, there was no place to hide.

"I can tell you're not happy," he told me, putting his hand over mine. "What's the problem?"

"Oh, nothing surprising," I said, trying to fend off the attention. "You know, just the usual. I haven't exactly achieved my goals. I'm not a famous writer and I never ended up with the love of my life. I'm looking at old age coming my way, and I can't get an agent or a boyfriend."

He squeezed my hand. "Stop feeling sorry for yourself and do something about it."

I shrugged and forced a smile. "Right."

"Here's what I want you to do. You know that little bar in Wallingford called Changes?"

"Wait a sec, okay. I think I know the one you mean." This was before I'd been there with Jordan. "That itsy-bitsy little gay bar? I thought it went out of business a long time ago. Is it still there?"

"Yes, it's still there," he said, with a tolerant smile. "It's been there for almost seventeen years, and it's a very nice little bar. Walk up there, it's not that far – what is it, a couple miles?"

"Alone?" I objected. "I don't think so. Why would I want to go to a bar by myself? That doesn't sound like fun. It sounds miserable."

Changes

"By yourself," he said firmly. "You go in, you drink one drink slowly, and you watch and you listen and you talk to at least one person, and then you can walk home. That's how you leave yourself open to the universe. Otherwise, you're going to get an earful from me personally."

It was a challenge I couldn't ignore. I had to do it at least once. Going there with Jordan had alleviated some of the fearsomeness of the place. So here I was, striding toward Changes, facing my own solitude, walking there alone.

It was a classic hot summer night, a night when anything can happen. From where I live down in Ravenna Springs, I walked up the hill to the University District, past the fraternities and sororities and then out the main avenue through the business district toward the bridge over the freeway. That night the usual headlight beams and fluorescent shop signs lit up 45th but all the bright lights in Seattle couldn't dispel my premonitions.

What would I *do* in a small bar alone? What kind of guys went to drink somewhere by themselves? What kind of dreadful people with dreadful habits was I about to encounter? I began walking slower and slower.

My high anxiety level exaggerated everything around me into omens of disaster.

As I was crossing the Ave, sirens started wailing. A fire truck rounded the turn by the Neptune Theater. As I got to the corner, I could count seven fire engines congesting the street

Changes

around the Safeco Tower, lights flashing, as though they were braced for a terrorist attack, an apocalyptic nuclear threat, firemen looking up at the tower's height, ready for a deadly menace, a circle of huge ominous red beasts alert to the scent of death.

I'd hardly walked two blocks farther down to Roosevelt Way when I heard shouting and drunken cries, belligerent and aggressive. It sounded like a brawl. Coming down 45th straight toward me was the source of the noise – an open-bed truck full of belligerent men howling for trouble.

Were they right-wing fundamentalists? Anti-black, anti-Jew, anti-gay? My panicky impulse to bolt down a side street was checked when I took another look at their clothes.

They were Seafair pirates.

Just a truck-bed packed with rambunctious men on their way to some parade, shouting and blowing their cannon and waving imitation swords.

My pounding heart embarrassed me. How butch was that, to be scared by a bunch of clowns in pirate suits? But it was one of those magic nights when the universe seems to be trying to tell you something you're too stupid to understand. Comforted that no one had seen my panic, I left the University District behind, continuing on across the freeway bridge above the rumbling, streaming river of headlights and up two more hills into the Wallingford neighborhood.

My reluctant walking speed decreased even more. I had stretched a half-hour walk into forty-five minutes. Fifteen

Changes

extra minutes of sheer anxiety. I was a tense mess. My legs were crippled with dread.

And then the walk was over. I could put it off no longer. I was there. I was at Changes. I was standing on the sidewalk in front of the black door.

It's a small and unobtrusive place, far from the gay district, on a block dominated by two big movie theaters with blazing marquees, sandwiched between a pizza house and a Thai restaurant. You could walk right past it without noticing. Nothing about it demands to be noticed. It's small and flat and black, and only the word CHANGES over the door would give you a clue it was anything at all and not just an extension of something else.

Of course, once you notice it, then you see the sign warning away minors, not to mention two rainbow flags on either side of the name and two fluorescent beer logos in the windows, which give a few clues to the nature of the clientele. To the outside world, the windows reveal only an occasional glimpse of a spatula flipping burgers on a grill. Whether it's crowded full of men or nearly empty, the little bar looks the same from the sidewalk. You can't tell what you'll find inside until you tug open the door.

The door won't tug open.

That's the first surprise. It only opens if you push, and then it swings inward unexpectedly easy with an announcing, bar-filling creak. Everyone in the bar turns to see who comes in. They can't help it. That creaking sound means this could be

Changes

Prince Charming arriving at last. A dozen faces, two dozen faces – or maybe only seven – turn hopefully to see if all the waiting has finally paid off, if the guy who's been missing from their life has finally arrived.

It's only me.

Yes, I'm a bit tense. I'm not exactly over-confident. I'm no knockout. I'm presentable. I mean, you wouldn't call me handsome, but if you were in a good mood you might call me attractive. I've learned the kind of impact I make on gay men. I provoke a flicker of curiosity, a raised eyelid, a glance that lingers just a flicker too long. But that about covers it. I've got two big aces, one in my shorts and one in my skull, but neither of them shows until later.

That's why I was at Changes. Maybe I'd do better in a smaller bar, in friendlier surroundings, with fewer pretty young competitors.

So there I was. No matter how unobtrusive I tried to be, the creaking caused all eyes to turn and regard me. The lights were dim, but several dozen people were scattered through the bar. I looked right past them. No one seemed to be talking. Had they stopped because of me? Even the music had paused. Things were too quiet.

The interior consisted mainly of that one long bar, with a dimly-lit cavern stretching the length of it. With men seated at the bar on the left and men clustered around three high tables on the right, I made my way down to where the bartender stood in front of the cash register. Each step of the

Changes

way was one more step alone. I was doing it. I was going into a gay bar all by myself. If I hadn't been so nervous, I might have noticed how odd it was that no one was shooting balls at the pool table, which was covered and strangely glowing in floodlights at the end of the bar.

"What can I get you?" said the handsome bald guy behind the bar.

"Long Island," I said quickly. I'd need something potent to get me through this.

I recognized the bartender, the big shoulders and head shaved bare. His dark blue T-shirt clung to his torso nicely.

I only had a ten-dollar bill. He turned away to open the change drawer.

A burst of music, and various customers started clapping. Someone shouted "Earl," someone else seconded the cry, but no one named Earl stepped forward. Not until the bartender turned around to give me the rest of my money did I realize he was holding a mike to his lips.

"Let – me – entertain – you," he belted out in a full, bold tenor, catching me totally by surprise, "let me make you smile." Holding up the mike cord, Earl came around from behind the bar singing, lingering by my stool to sing the next few bars. "And if you're real good, I'll make you feel good," he crooned, and gave me a poke in the ribs as he moved past me, taking command of the bar as he stepped into the theatrical lighting in front of the pool table.

I had walked into the middle of karaoke night.

Changes

One by one that night they all came forward to sing, the regulars, the lifeblood of the bar, the strangers that I would soon know well, Buster and Shawn, Colby and Jude, as though I had stepped into a musical and each character was called by name to sing their number. For just a moment, in that small neighborhood bar, I left behind the everyday world where people were only capable of speech. I found myself in a new and exalted universe where the denizens sang, a happier dimension of reality.

I was determined to make it my own.

Changes

KING OF THE SEAS

You can face your fear of rejection, you can go into a gay bar alone, but unless it's karaoke night it doesn't mean anyone's going to burst into song when you walk through the door. Daring to cross the threshold and drink your drink doesn't mean you'll connect with one single person.

The first visit to Changes was easy.

The second visit was a disaster. Later I would learn that on Saturdays the neighborhood folk often venture farther from home, treating themselves to one of the discos downtown or pretty-boy bars in the gay district. Those few guys in Changes that Saturday night had clearly known each other for years. They didn't know me at all.

I was the only one drinking alone. I gulped down my Long Island and teetered out.

Walking home, I decided that I'd given this whole bar thing a fair chance, but it just wasn't for me. I felt worse coming out than I had going in. I wouldn't waste any more time on it. I don't enjoy drinking that much. I don't watch television or sports or music videos. I don't like sitting around unless I've got a book in my hands. The place was unnatural for me. I was a critter out of his element. No wonder no one talked to me. They could sense I didn't belong there.

Changes

I sulked all the way home, my thoughts growing darker and darker. My preconceptions about trying to break into gay society had been completely corroborated. Gay people simply didn't accept me. I'd spent most of my life in various states of sexual adoration over straight guys, the yell king, the varsity wrestler, the Navy cadet, the car mechanic, the pilot, the gambler, the entrepreneur, guys with macho credentials who also had a wild side. I was the pursuer, the worshipper. The price of my one-way sexuality was that I'd long ago lost all sense of my own physical presence and needs. I didn't know my own sexual identity. I was completely in the dark.

Going to a gay bar by myself was intended to help. It was supposed to center me in my own body so that I could be a gay man among equals. Instead it only proved to me what I already knew, that all the other ducklings could tell I didn't belong in the nest, that I was a goose, not a duck. Gay guys weren't my brothers. Straight guys were my doom. Something in my sexual trigger was defective, and it fired chasing after the ones who didn't want me, the cocky ones with the masculine chemistry I couldn't perceive in myself, a long, disastrous chain of jocks and jerks who were willing to accept all the adoration they could get. My romances over the decades had resulted in a little army of straight guys who broke the rules with me.

The straight guy who lasted the longest was Tom Webber, and on that cold, bright Sunday afternoon before I

Changes

went to Changes for the third time, I decided to phone him to wish him a happy birthday.

Ordinarily that would have been impossible. Tom's phone was disconnected two years ago for lack of payment. But I knew the number of the drug rehabilitation center in British Columbia where he was currently taking a two-month break from his frenetic crack addiction.

I had no illusions. He'd soon be back in Seattle handing over his paycheck to his drug dealers, begging for change in the shopping malls and eating charity meals in churches. But for now, he was locked down and getting three square meals a day. Maybe he'd be sober enough to appreciate a birthday wish from the only long-term friend in his life.

Do I sound cold? It's the only way I can talk about him. I thought he was the one for life. I won't let myself feel any more for him. I can't save him.

The Canadian fellow at the drug abuse center who answered the phone listened patiently and politely to my request. Then he assured me he couldn't confirm that such a person as Tom Webber was currently at that institute. Nor could he confirm that the birthday wish would be delivered. I sighed. So much for that idea.

I was surprised half an hour later to receive a phone call from Tom, crackly with distance. He had not received my message. He'd simply had exactly the same thought, to remind me that it was his birthday. Since he'd been given a half-hour

Changes

of phone time, he was including me in his calls to the free world.

"It's awful here," he said. "All they say to you all day long is 'Surrender, surrender, surrender.' I don't surrender. I'm not the type."

That was for sure.

"They all say I'm the stubborn one," he laughed.

"Get as much as you can out of it, buddy," I wished him. We both pretended that he was committed to benefiting from his treatment, pretended that his lawyer brothers weren't wasting $11,000, pretended that Tom really wanted to change. Tom isn't interested in change. He's into fearless headlong disaster. He's a high wire artist addicted to tempting his luck, the clerk who can't keep his hand out of the till, the Russian roulette guy who's determined to cash out.

I try to be tough and I *am* tough and I'm over him, but I was still crying as I hung up the phone. Then I flipped open the phone book, found the number I was looking for, and punched in the number.

"Changes," said the busy voice on the other end.

"Say, um, can you help me, I'm sorta new," I faltered, not making any sense. I started over. "What's the best time to come tonight?"

"Tonight's karaoke," said the voice, warmer. "Come around 9:30. Things should be hopping."

Changes

Maybe not exactly hopping, but things were certainly livelier than Saturday. After a brisk walk through the crisp, chilly night, the warm bar was welcoming and the singing had already begun. The three tables in front were all crowded, and every stool was taken along the bar.

A house-rocking torch song was in progress. A knot of laughing guys clogged the aisle between the dartboard and the coolers. The sound system was rigged in front of the pool table. Two middle-aged lesbians with slicked-back hair and matching leather jackets were singing passionately sad songs to each other, drunkenly professing their love.

I got my Long Island and tried to back myself into a place where I could see the performers as well as check out the other guys in the bar.

One guy was an immediate standout, quickly and completely capturing my attention no matter how much I tried to look away. He was the best-looking guy in the house, a flat, lean blond with a flashy smile and showy body, wearing a white T-shirt that showed just enough. His back was turned to me, while he lavished attention on several guys at the bar, apparently his friends.

I tried to hear what he was saying, and couldn't. I tried feebly to ignore him, and then just gave in. Between watching a pool game, watching a rock video on multiple screens, or watching an attractive guy in a short T-shirt, the choice is an easy one, especially when he doesn't appear to notice.

Changes

Which is why I'm caught so completely off-guard when he turns around and walks straight up to me and says, "And who might you be?"

When I regain my wits and my voice, I tell him my name.

"I'm Nathan," he says, shaking my hand warmly. "Nathan Gold." He takes a step closer and says, "Would you mind if I asked you a question?" and as he says it, he touches one finger to the center of my chest.

I nod lamely. "Fire away."

"I just feel I can ask you this," says Nathan. "I know it's personal, but if you can, be honest." He looks me dead-on in the eye, stepping forward to get out of someone's way and bumping up against me. "How do you feel about yourself as a gay man?"

That takes the wind out of me. My brain goes into overload, and all I can draw are blanks. What do you say when someone seems to be reading your mind? Do you turn around and run straight out the door?

"I like myself as a gay man," I say defensively, immediately, without thinking, then add, "but now that I'm older, well, in gay society I've become a second-class citizen. I mean, I've said goodbye to my forties. I don't have strong, stupid youth to offer anymore. It's like running lower and lower on money in the gay shopping mall. I'm starting to do a lot of window-shopping."

Changes

"I appreciate your honesty." He gives my shoulder an affectionate squeeze. "You look to me like you've still got a lot of life left in you. Okay, now let me ask you this." He gestures broadly like an Italian opera star, opening his arms to include everyone in the bar as well as show off the supple firmness under his T-shirt. "Do you feel the equal of the people in this bar?"

This guy is making me uneasy, but I'm fascinated. "I'm totally intimidated by everybody here," I confess bluntly. "Everyone seems to know what they're doing here but me."

He wrinkles up his nose quizzically, like he doesn't quite believe me. "Do you feel part of the gay community?"

"No," I said. "Gay people all seem to know each other. I feel like I'm not quite officially gay, not an authentic card-carrying member."

"Too bad," he says, gripping my shoulder again. "Sorry to hear that. We should all feel like we belong. How about in terms of all the people in Seattle?"

To get out of a passing man's way, Nathan moves forward until he's pressed up against me. His face is a couple inches away. This is all too good to be true. What am I doing right? I try to focus on what I'm saying, and not on all the current points of physical contact.

"Do you feel like you're an equal member of the Seattle community?"

Changes

I'm willing to talk to this guy about anything, but really, couldn't we move on to a more personal topic? But he asked for honesty, and I tried to give it to him.

"Well, I mean, I'm free to think I'm equal, I'm not actively oppressed," I qualify, "but I'm certainly not an actual equal in Seattle. I mean, I'm gay, and we can't do some things. Obviously we can't marry. We can't even walk around holding hands without sooner or later attracting hostility. In most of our professional lives we have to pretend to be straight. Hiding is part of being gay. Well, hiding isn't equality."

"Yes, yes, yes," he says, giving me a fond cuff on the side of the head. "Exactly. You've got it right. You're beautiful, man." He's so close I can smell him, and he smells like soap and guy. "So, how do we get equality?" He puts his hand on my shoulder, as though to help me find the answer.

"Change," I manage to say. "Political change."

I think he's going to kiss me. "Exactly."

I'm having an intelligent conversation with a stunning young man who appears genuinely interested in me, who's smart enough to understand what I'm saying and bright enough to ask questions. Suddenly the two-mile walk to Changes seems worth it.

"Well, one thing's for sure," he breathes on me. "Political change doesn't happen by dreaming about it." He emphasizes each word, touch and poke, touch and poke. He's playing me like a musical instrument, and each beat gets a

Changes

finger tap on my chest, a knuckle knock, a slap, a squeeze. "It's brought about by dedicated, hard-working brothers and sisters who aren't going to settle for less than equality."

Okay, I'll sign up. I'll pay. I'll march. I'll do whatever I have to do to keep getting thumped like this. Just show me the dotted line.

"So," he says, impulsively giving me a one-armed hug, "I just want you to know something." Nathan practically bumps his nose into mine. "I'm in a position to fight for that equality. I've been elected to represent you. And that's exactly what I'll be doing now for one year. I'll be fighting for your rights." He pounds his fist on my chest like a gavel of justice. "I'm working for equal legislation and representation for all gay people in Seattle. And I want you to know something else. I'm straight."

My mouth slowly falls open. "You're what?"

"I'm straight," he says with a wink, "but very gay friendly. And last night I became the first straight guy in the thirty years of the gay community's Imperial Court of Seattle to be voted King of the Seas."

He went on, but he'd lost me. I had gone quietly into shock. I remember watching his handsome jaw moving. I was so close I could count every pore, every stubble. I remember watching that dinky white T-shirt doing such a poor job of keeping his body covered.

Changes

He was telling me about the different fund-raisers he'd be sponsoring when I pulled down my jacket off the coat rack and said good-night.

I walked out of the bar doubting myself. Was it something about me? Could it just be coincidence that I'd been attracted like a suicidal moth to the one straight guy in a gay bar? A roaring river of metal flowed beneath me, a torrent of headlights, as I crossed the freeway bridge heading home.

Changes

THE THIRD BATHROOM

It was a new world, and like all new worlds it had mysteries to be penetrated.

Night by night, week by week, I explored the little bar. I discovered its habits and its strategies. The tables by the door were a place where it was easy to get trapped alone. The bench beyond the pool table was a hard place to reach if guys were playing pool. Most of the regulars sat on stools at the bar. The loudest talkers gathered at the bar's south end. Many of the customers had previous relationships. They greeted each other by name. They kissed and hugged and groped and teased, and knew things about each other I couldn't guess.

The bar had rhythms. Sometimes it was full, sometimes down to only three or four guys. Some nights were for pool, some nights were for karaoke, some nights were for grilling burgers or steaks. The price of my Long Island would constantly fluctuate depending on the bartender, each calculating by unguessable rules. One of the four bartenders even made the drink smaller than the others. I pointed that out to him. Later I found out he was the owner.

Changes

My first hesitant visits to Changes presented me with dozens of questions, but none so oddly compelling as the afternoon I discovered the bar had three bathrooms.

It was August by then, and the afternoon had been a wrenching one. My ex-lover had called from the clinic for drug abuse in British Columbia where his brothers had committed him. He was resisting treatment. He had contempt for his doctors. He was halfway through a two-month therapy plan, hating and wasting every minute of it.

"It's boot camp for drug addicts," he complained.

"At least you're getting three meals a day." He had been living on pancake batter. "Try to be open, buddy. Try to learn something. Please."

He hung up on me.

"Honey, you need to get out," said Brad, putting his arm around me up in the bookstore Returns area where he worked. "When you're depressed, the best thing in the world for you is – food." He patted the red apron that covered his ample girth. "So let's go get some tonight."

I accepted. That night I would *not* go to Changes. I would be going to dinner with a dear friend, who would help me discuss the pain of watching a man I loved trapped in the nightmare of crack addiction, fighting against the treatment that could save his life.

Brad often takes me out to dinner. He and I bonded the day we met. We're book people. He's the only man I know who has more books than I do and actually reads them. With

Changes

his fluffy white beard, buzzcut head and considerable girth, he looks like Santa's punk younger brother. A college dropout, Brad educated himself through sheer book passion, knows his Victorians cold, and ran a gay bookstore in San Francisco for eight years. He's kind and respectful to all varieties of human life. He's a leaky, spurting faucet of love.

That afternoon I walked up and met him at the bookstore on the Ave. From there we walked to his car in a lot three blocks away.

"So, have you decided what you want for dinner?" he began, as he always began. As I always replied, I replied, "Wherever you feel like eating is fine with me. I'm in it for the company."

"Okay, which do you like best," he asked, as we pulled out of the parking lot, "Thai or Vietnamese?"

"Whichever one has the most peanut sauce."

We had drifted to other subjects when I noticed he was driving toward Wallingford. "So, which one did you choose?"

"Didn't you say that Tuesdays were $1.50 burger-and-fries at Changes?"

That caught me by surprise. "So they say. The bartender says Tuesday is the best day of the week."

"Well, dear, it's Tuesday. What are we waiting for?"

So I was going to Changes, after all. We circled through tree-lined Wallingford neighborhood streets until we found a parking spot, and walked to the bar. We were at the

Changes

stoplight, waiting to cross, when I saw at the stoplight one block up from us a totally stunning blond guy in a tight white tanktop who was just crossing the street.

"My God, look at that sexy straight guy," I couldn't help but say. "What a hunk. The way they walk. Like they own the world."

Brad laughed at me. "That's a lesbian, you idiot."

I looked again. "No way," I protested.

But now I wasn't so sure. I'd mistaken lesbians for sexy men before. I hate it when that happens. I checked him out again. He walked like a man. He had shoulders like a man. And that tanktop fit him oh so well. But could he be a lesbian? From that distance, I couldn't be sure. Was it possible that gender mattered so much if it could be so hard to tell?

We pushed open the door into a packed tavern, lively and noisy, and it was still early. We ordered our burgers, paid for them, and sat down on the bench beyond the pool table to nurse our drinks.

"It's a tad dark in here," observed Brad. Our eyes were still adjusting. "Feels like we've come from the daylight world of the Eloi into the underground world of the Morlocks."

Brad always talks like that. Book talk.

True, the small window at the front of the bar provided almost no light for the rest of it. The August sun couldn't reach us here, but after the first few sips of my Long Island, I didn't really care. More and more people arrived. The place was hopping. And as Brad and I sat over by ourselves on the

Changes

pool bench, watching the rest of the bar comport itself, one of the mysteries of Changes presented itself.

"Where does that door go?" asked Brad, pointing over by the coat rack.

"It's a bathroom," I said. "I assume. Guys come out of it adjusting their zippers, so it must be."

"Well, how about that door?" He pointed across the pool table, toward the corner.

"Another bathroom. I think that one's for women, though everybody uses it. I think they keep the mop and stuff in there, too."

"Well then, how about that door?" He pointed past the rack for pool cues.

"Isn't that just for management?"

"Of course not," he said. "Haven't you seen guys go in there and come out of there?"

"Well, I always thought it was a bathroom, too. Funny, I never added them all up before. I don't notice bathrooms. I guess there are three."

Brad laughed. "There can't be three bathrooms."

That a bar as small as Changes would have two bathrooms seemed a luxury. That it would have three seemed absurd, and yet that appeared to be the case. The mystery of the third bathroom was one I wasn't very well equipped to solve, since I generally avoid public bathrooms, especially gay ones. Something about having my sexual equipment exposed and vulnerable and my back to the door makes me too

Changes

uncomfortable to pee. So I was vaguely aware of the bathrooms, I knew they were there. But I had never ventured into them.

Then a couple of cute guys came out of the third bathroom that we hadn't seen before.

"Where the hell did *they* come from?" said Brad.

I was wondering the same thing. "They must have been in there an awfully long time."

"They've been in there since before we got here," he pointed out.

"Are you thinking what I'm thinking?" I hoped he wasn't. I was remembering the notorious private sex rooms of the Seventies, where a kind of bathhouse abandon took place in taverns on the other side of an unmarked door, bondage and water sports and who knew what all.

"Well, honey," said Brad, patting my knee, "we're never going to find out just sitting here."

"Um, I don't feel like walking in on an orgy, thank you. Let's just wait here for our burgers in happy ignorance."

"I can't believe you've never checked it out."

"I never go to the bathroom in bars."

"Here come two more. That bathroom has got to be bigger than the other two, because at least six guys – no seven –have come out of there that we didn't see go in." Brad slid off the bench. "I'm going in there. Wanna come?"

"I don't need to pee."

Changes

"It's got nothing to do with peeing. I want to know what goes on in there."

I definitely didn't want to know. I grabbed his arm. "Don't, Brad. What if they ask us to leave? What if it's only for certain customers?" In reaching for him, I'd inadvertently slipped to my feet as well. I found myself following him reluctantly. "This is not a good idea."

When he reached for the doorknob, I took a step backward. He tugged the door open. There was a blaze of light. I squinted in amazement, as we stepped outdoors.

"Just like Dorothy stepping out of the crashed farmhouse into Oz," said Brad. I followed, and the door thudded behind me.

It was a small patio, too tiny to be called a courtyard, with only room for three non-matching tables. A dozen happy people were crowded around them talking, laughing, and munching their burgers and fries.

"Who would have guessed?" he exclaimed. "We've just stepped out of Plato's cave into the sunlight of reality."

Suddenly big, muscular Earl appeared before us like a bald genie balancing several platters of burgers and offering two of them to us. Fortunately Brad noticed a bench over on the side where we might just fit. "Come on, let's have a seat. We can't eat these standing up."

As I sit down beside him, I discover to my amazement that I'm sitting right behind the very same lesbian with peroxide hair and a white tanktop. She looks just as much like

Changes

a hunky guy now from the back as she did from one block down and across the street. She's got shoulders like a guy. She's got biceps like a guy. No wonder I thought she was a guy. She laughs, and the sound is pure masculinity.

"My, my, my, these are really quite tasty," says Brad, halfway through his burger.

The peroxide lesbian hears him, and with a fist full of burger and a cheek full of bite, turns around and says, "Aren't they incredible?"

She *is* a guy.

I'm going into shock, but Brad isn't. He's a fountain of wit, with a bon mot and a juicy riposte for every comment from the other table. Before I've taken a bite of my burger, we've been included in the ongoing conversation.

In the midst of it all, the former lesbian reaches out his hand and introduces himself to me as Ray. He's had enough beers that he's very free with his hands, and they're all over me. He's in his late thirties, with a sweetly-maintained body and a very conscious tan. When he glances at his watch and rises to his feet to leave, Ray gives me a kiss and says he comes to Changes often and looks forward to seeing me again.

By the time I come back to earth, Brad has everyone at our table laughing at something I missed. I look at them questioningly, waiting to hear what's so funny, and they laugh harder. Turns out they were laughing at me.

We finished our burgers, finished our beers, and knew everyone's name at our table before Brad announced it was

Changes

time for him to get home to his hubby. Stepping out of the fading afternoon back into the dim light of the tavern, it was already hard to remember a time when we didn't know the patio was there.

As we made our way down the length of the bar, I grabbed him by the shoulder and finally had to ask him. "Brad, why did you tell me that Ray was really a woman?"

"I didn't."

"Yes, you did. You said he was a lesbian."

Brad shook his head and clucked at me sadly. "You're so tragically literal. It's just a term, dear. It means a butch guy who's really a lady."

I sighed. It didn't really matter. "What a great night."

"A totally charming night," he said, pulling open the tavern door back out to the street. "I feel like one of those adventurers in a Jules Verne novel who has just discovered a whole other world."

"Come on, Captain Nemo. I'm tuckered out. I want to go to bed."

Our dinner gamble had paid off grandly in pure pleasure. Unfortunately, our pleasure was about to exact a price. I think the question occurred to both of us at the same time as we stood on the curb, waiting for the light to change.

"Where exactly did we park?" asks Brad.

Those are words no passenger wants to hear. "I didn't notice, really. I was trusting that you did."

Changes

"Hmmm, this isn't good," he groaned. "The Trojan War may be over, but Odysseus isn't home yet."

Tipsy and tired, the two of us set off for where we thought his car was parked. It wasn't.

We tried up a street.

We tried down a street.

And so the night swallowed us, as we wandered through the dark neighborhoods of Wallingford, searching quiet little streets all lined with trees that looked exactly alike, pooped and drunk and giggling at our own stupidity, block after block, hunting and hoping.

Changes

FATHERS AND SONS

That evening Dad stopped by my place on his way back from Calvary Cemetery. He'd gone to leave flowers freshly cut from his garden on his mother's grave. He's eighty but spry, prides himself on his health. He was wearing the new suspenders I gave him for his birthday. I could tell he didn't like seeing me having ramen noodles for dinner.

"That's not all you're eating, is it?"

"Actually it's very filling."

"Can't you do better than that?"

"Things are just a little tight this week, Dad," I explained. "The heel broke on my shoe. Had to buy a new pair. It was just an extra hundred dollars I didn't happen to have. It's no big deal. I get paid Tuesday."

He didn't believe me. Long after he left I went into the bathroom to brush my teeth. With my mouth full of suds I noticed in the mirror that something green was sticking out of one corner of the medicine cabinet, like the message in a fortune cookie. It was a twenty dollar bill.

That sweet father of mine!

Impulsively I decided to celebrate my new wealth by walking up to Changes. Just one drink, and the rest of the money would be for groceries on the way home.

Changes

The front door of the bar had been propped open to lure in the occasional breath of fresh air. Though we were halfway through September, the sun was still fighting through the clouds and the air was hot and muggy. From the sidewalk I could peek through the doorway. All I could see was a long empty bar with two people at the end of it.

I pulled back, not so sure I felt like going inside. I could save my money, turn around and walk back home. Then I noticed that Earl, my favorite bartender, was on duty, and decided that a Long Island iced tea would make my walk home that much easier.

Not until after placing my drink order did I notice that one of the guys beside me wasn't in very good shape. His arms were folded on the bar, and his face was trying to burrow down into them, so all you could see was the back of a nearly bald head, a sweaty neck, the noose of a loosened tie, and the rumpled back of his threadbare jacket.

"Is he okay?" I asked Earl, dropping a bill in the tip bowl.

Earl shook his bald head and was trying to mouth something to me when the guy sitting on the other side of him turned around.

"You gotta excuse my friend," he said. "He's having a real hard night." He came over to stand beside me and extended his hand. "My name's Jude."

I told him mine. I'd seen him there before. I always thought of him as Caribbean, a handsome black guy about

Changes

forty, with an Arabic nose, black jewels for eyes, and a lean physique beginning to bulk out with beer. Suddenly he began shoving his hands in his pockets, searching for something. He was about to shout when he saw what he was looking for behind him on the bar counter. Slamming his hand down on a piece of paper, he slid it toward me.

"You haven't seen this kid, have you?"

The limp, folded sheet had clearly been shown to many people before me. It was a reproduction of a smiling kid's face, all cheeks and freckles, his melon-round head a little too large, his smile a little too broad.

I shook my head. "Is something wrong?"

He misunderstood my question. "He's retarded."

"He's not retarded," barked a voice from the pile of arms on the counter. I still couldn't see his friend's face, but I didn't much want to. The voice was soggy with phlegm and tears, and I imagined his face was not a pretty sight. "I told you, he's not retarded, he's challenged."

"Okay, you know what I mean." Jude dug his fingers down scratching into the fuzzy black dreads clustered all over his head in little spikes. "The thing is he's not real smart."

"He's a genius," corrected the voice in the folded arms.

"What I'm trying to say," said Jude patiently, "is the kid does the same thing every day, and as long as he does it the same way every time, exactly the same, everything is okay. But today he didn't follow his routine. He didn't get on the 2:45 bus."

Changes

His words gave me a chill. I was starting to understand the wretchedness of his friend. "Where did he go?" I asked.

"Nobody knows," said Jude, and I was starting to see how much sadness there was in his eyes. "Nobody's seen him. My pal here is going crazy."

"I've been searching for him," said his friend, raising his head halfway up out of his sleeves on the counter. Now I could see his eyes, faded watery blue, like they'd run out of color. "I drove down every street around his school. Every street. The alleys, too. The police made me go home. They said they would get hold of me as soon as they found him."

The phone rang, startling all of us.

The guy lunged to his feet, clawed out his cell phone and clutched it like a lifeline to his mouth. "Yeah, yeah?" He was in his late thirties, bony and losing his hair, with a faltering little fringe beard outlining his weak jaw. Inhibited and awkward in dealing with us, he was clearly a man most comfortable at home.

He listened intently to the tiny voice. His features fell, the air went out of him. "Yeah, that's probably it. That must have been it. Thanks," he said, and hung up. "That was the principal. There was some kind of fight after school. Two boys were suspended. Nothing serious, but it must have freaked Simon. One of the kids got a bloody nose. Simon is very upset by violence."

"Do they have any idea where he might be?"

Changes

"They just know he didn't get on his bus. But he's not on the school grounds anywhere. He never misses his bus. He hates change."

"Would his friends maybe know where he is?" I asked. "Do the other kids like him?"

When I saw the look on his face, I regretted asking. "Oh, you know kids. Some like him. Some are scared of him. He's got two little buddies. But sure, he takes some hassling. That comes with the territory, doesn't it?"

"How's his mother taking it?"

A look of quiet defiance hardened his gaze. "There's no mother in this story," he said with finality. "I'm it."

"And he's the best father you ever saw," said Jude aggressively in my face as though I might possibly be harboring doubts. "There is no father in that school who would do more than he does for Simon."

"He's my boy," said the miserable man, gnawing at the back of a fingernail. "He's just lost somewhere, and scared. He'll be all right. It's just hard when it happens, that's all, it's just hard. But he'll be fine. He's always fine."

He was talking to himself, not believing a word. I sucked at my straws, and discovered that half of my drink was already gone.

The second time the phone rang, his fingers were so frantic that he fumbled getting it out of his pocket. It clattered to the floor. I snatched it up, but before I could give it to him he ripped it out of my hand.

Changes

"Yeah? This is he. Yes, I'm his father." As he listened, the tension slowly ebbed from his face, replaced by exhaustion and relief. "And he's okay?" He listened, his mouth trembling with one emotion after another. "Oh, sure, of course." His smile was quivering on the edge of tears. "Right. Right away. Fifteen minutes." Mumbling his gratitude, he clicked off his cell.

"He's at the Kirkland Park-and-Ride," he explained, and downed the rest of his drink in one motion. "He's fine." His empty glass came down heavily on the bar, but he was too happy to notice. "He was so scared by the fight at school that he got on the wrong bus. He was crying, obviously lost. The bus driver called the police. Here." He shoved a wad of bills toward Earl. "Thanks, you guys."

"Phone me and tell me how he is," Jude called after him.

"I'm not phoning you," the man called back as he dashed down the length of the bar. "I can't afford to call Pittsburgh. You call me."

He bolted out the door, knocking aside the door prop so that the door whooshed shut behind him, sealing us into a hot tomb of motionless air.

"That boy means everything to him," said Jude, watching after his friend for a moment longer. "You never saw a father like that guy. And the boy knows it. They love each other, those two. You should see 'em." He shook his head and smiled over memories he was savoring. "The court tried to

Changes

take the kid away from him when his wife left. Said no gay man should be raising a kid like Simon alone. Well, they got a piece of his mind, all right," Jude chuckled. "It's a lucky boy has a father like that, damned lucky."

"So, I don't understand," I decided to ask, "why did he say that he couldn't call you in Pittsburgh?"

"Oh, that's my fault," he said, draining his glass of beer. "My cell phone is listed in Pittsburgh. That's where my Daddy lives. He pays the bill. That's why anybody who calls me in Seattle has to call long distance." He poured himself another glass of beer. "My father couldn't stand being out of touch with me." He faltered awkwardly. "Sometimes I'm not very good with money. Sometimes I – well, I didn't pay my phone bill. It got disconnected. He couldn't reach me. He hated that."

He turned back to his glass of beer, peering into the yellow depths and brooding over unpaid phone bills. I said good-night and headed for the University District to buy groceries with the rest of my father's money.

Changes

JEALOUS BOYFRIEND

A neighborhood tavern can become your second home.

I went there on Sundays and Wednesdays to watch the regulars singing karaoke. I went there on Tuesdays because cheap burgers and cheap beer brought in the biggest and happiest and friendliest crowds of the week. Mondays had free pool. Saturdays had free darts. Sunday afternoons had an all-you-can-eat brunch.

The ebb and flow of the bar became the tide of my life.

I was still a stranger at Changes no matter how often I went. I was still the guy no one knew. I might see a look of recognition flicker in a young pool player's eyes. Jude the black Caribbean might greet me. I might get a smile and a pat from the short karaoke host as he hustled back and forth setting up his sound equipment. But no one knew my name. No one knew who I was, where I came from, or why I was coming there.

That all changed one night in August.

Earl was bartending. I ordered my usual. He poured four bottles at once into my Long Island, two bottles in each hand, just another of those butch displays of confidence that took my breath away.

Drink in hand, I set off for my spot.

Changes

After my first few visits, trying out different areas in the little tavern, sitting at one of the tables, or on a stool at the bar, or on the bench by the pool table, or in the shadows of the patio, I'd finally found my particular place, the place that seemed right for me. It was standing against the wall by the coat rack, right where the going gets tight between the bar and the coolers, just before the room widens to accommodate the pool table. That was the best vantage point in the middle of the bar to see in both directions, and especially for watching karaoke or pool. Then I improved it by hauling myself up out of the way onto the metal bench above the coolers, where I could rest my shoulders between the pull-tab machines and comfortably settle back.

Jude was sitting on a stool at the bar in front of me. He turned half-around to face me, with an admiring nod of his dreadlocks in Earl's direction, somehow intuiting that I was also fascinated by the bartender. "What I like about Earl, he's a masculine guy, know what I mean?"

Earl was clearly the macho icon of the little tavern. His solid build, snug T-shirts, guy's arms, guy's voice, all contributed toward the living sexual flavor of the bar. That handsome shaved head, that butch handling of the bottles behind the bar, it was all part of the show.

Jude was about to say something else when he scowled at me. "Why the hell are you sitting up there? Come on down here."

Changes

Finally someone at Changes was asking for my company. Though I was reluctant to abandon my spot, I was only too glad to be invited. I swung my legs down from the metal bench and climbed onto the bar stool next to him.

"He used to be married," said Jude, nodding his dreadlocks toward Earl. "Then he went to jail. I think it was for armed robbery. Then he finally figured out he was gay three years ago. Look at him. Now that's a man."

Jude told me a little about himself. He was a truck driver for an Italian restaurant chain, the only employee who didn't have to know how to make pizzas. That exception made him laugh in delight. All he had to do was drive the truck.

His real dream, the reason he'd come to Seattle, was to sing in a band. "Music is the love of my life. Too bad I can only do it when I'm drunk," he said. "My father was a professor of music."

He lingered in clear distress over his current unhappy situation at home. His roommate was in love with him, wouldn't move out, wouldn't pay rent, but cooked his meals, washed and cleaned, and scowled at the men he brought home. Jude's repeated orders to move out had no effect.

He was about to tell me more about this love-struck roommate when he was suddenly grabbed by two hairy blond forearms, hauled forward, and kissed on the lips. I recognized his assailant as French Fry.

How he got the nickname I never learned. He was a short bantam cock of a guy, all puffed out chest, who strutted around that bar like he owned it, frequently plowed, with enough blond stubble and beard for a Northern barbarian. Stringy yellow hair hung down the sides and back of his head in a weather-beaten fringe. He might have once had a hot body and he still had the ruins of a cute face, but hard living had given him a bit of a gut and the wasted look of someone who never found out that the party was over.

When their kiss finally ended and the two of them came up for air, Jude and French Fry included me in the general looks exchanged while they continued to embrace each other.

"Careful, he's here tonight," said French Fry.

"You should have warned me," said Jude, pulling away.

"I *am* warning you."

"I don't want him to cause a scene," said Jude.

"You know what he can be like." French Fry shuddered.

"His boyfriend is very jealous," said Jude, explaining. After a kiss like that, I thought French Fry's warning came a little late. Clearly his boyfriend had good reason for some healthy jealousy.

"Does he know you two like each other?"

"He hates me."

French Fry started kissing Jude again.

"Um, where exactly *is* this jealous boyfriend?"

Jude didn't hear me. They paused for breath, murmuring together, laughing. I figured they were dropping me a hint and tried to drift off to give them room, but Jude grabbed

Changes

my arm and pinned it to the bar. Clearly I was intended to stay. Finally, instead of just standing there grinning like a stump, I decided to participate in the conversation and also reveal the tiniest bit of knowledge that I'd managed to gather about the regulars at Changes.

"Why does everyone call you French Fry?" I said to him with a smile. After all, with a name like French Fry, it *had* to have a story.

Far from smiling to hear that I knew his affectionate nickname, he and Jude both looked at me in blank shock.

"What did you just say?" said French Fry.

I repeated my question. They looked at each other and back at me as though I'd lost my mind.

"No one calls me French Fry," he said slowly, studying my face.

"They don't?"

"They call me Viking."

"Viking?"

"Everybody calls me Viking."

"But..."

"Because I am one."

I was speechless. French Fry? How could I have been so off-base? And if I could be that wrong about his name, what other beliefs of mine were equally mistaken?

To my surprise, Jude and Viking went back to kissing.

"Um, you guys..."

Changes

I was getting extremely uncomfortable. Were they trying to get caught? Time for me to find some other company. I could go sit on the pool bench. I saw a free stool down at the end of the bar. Just how jealous was this boyfriend? And where exactly was he?

No one was glaring at us, ready to start breaking bones. There wasn't an angry-looking person in sight.

"Shit, he's coming," said Viking.

Which shows how wrong you can be. I immediately looked down at my drink, my stomach doing flip-flops. I concentrated on the ice cubes, trying to keep my hand steady, trying not to let the ice cubes tinkle nervously against the sides of the glass.

When I glanced up, Viking was gone.

"What happened?" I said to Jude. "Where'd he go?"

At any moment I expected a jealous boyfriend to appear out of nowhere and smack a fist into either one of us.

Jude drained his glass of beer. "Who?"

"Viking's jealous boyfriend."

"Probably giving Viking hell somewhere."

I felt sad and helpless. The conversation had nowhere to go. "Too bad. Say, I've been meaning to tell you, well, I've heard you sing at karaoke. You've got a beautiful voice."

"Yeah, and a lot of good it does me," he said, reaching for his jacket on the coat rack. "Come on, let's go out to the patio. It's a little cooler out there. You smoke?"

I shook my head.

Changes

"You ever go back there?"

"I don't really know anyone well enough to join them," I fumbled. "I, um, would feel weird back there all alone."

"Well, you're not alone with me."

He slid his arms into his jacket sleeves, adjusted the collar, and zipped it halfway up. He got almost to the patio door before he paused, and turned back just enough to give me an eye and a nod.

I jumped off my stool and followed him.

The patio was a little postage-stamp of darkness, surrounded by house-high walls but open to the night sky. It was like entering a small outdoor living room, with a tall mushroom-style heater sprouting in the center of it like a metal tree from outer space. The chattering mumble of laughter and voices in the dark slowly resolved, as my eyes got used to it, into shadowy figures in small clusters around three small, wobbly tables, drinking outside on one of the last warm evenings of the year.

Jude stopped suddenly. No tables were empty. He turned around and whispered something in a drunken slur that was completely incomprehensible, and I followed him toward the table by the trash bin gate. He looked at me and winked. I had no idea why.

Two people were already sitting there. They didn't seem to be saying much, and what little they did say stopped when we joined them. A stubby, very effeminate blond and a

Changes

quiet, handsome little fellow who looked Spanish were sharing the table.

"Do you mind if we join you?" asked Jude.

The Latin fellow rattled off something courteous. I couldn't tell whether it was Spanish or Spanglish, but his hand gesture made it clear we were welcome.

Jude and I slid onto the shadowy bench along the wall. There was just enough room, thigh to thigh, for us to fit.

As my eyes slowly adjusted to the dim light, I could make out other faces at the table next to ours, Colby the young pool shark, Anthony the singer, Buster the training barista. Here I am sitting with them, shoulder to shoulder.

That's the moment I realize I've been accepted. I'm in the back patio with the regulars. I've infiltrated this little community of brothers. I'm finally trusted. I'm one of them.

"A night like this, doesn't it make you think of Mahler's Ninth, the first movement?" says Jude, blowing out a stream of smoke into the dark.

"Mahler goes a little over my head," I admit. "I need more of a tune that I can whistle and hum."

"Mahler is my god," says Jude.

I try to tell him why I love Verdi and Mozart but don't understand Mahler or Puccini, when I realize Jude isn't really listening to me at all as much as staring at my face.

"You're really handsome," he says, making me feel instantly awkward. "I hope it doesn't bother you that I said that."

Changes

"I'm glad you like me," I fumble. "I'm the new guy. I want to be liked."

"You do know Mahler's Ninth at least, don't you?"

"Um, no."

Jude rises to his feet. "I've got a great recording of it at my place," he says, zipping up his jacket, waiting for me to respond to his invitation. When I don't, he continues briskly, adjusting his jacket collar, "Well, gotta get up early tomorrow morning."

He gives me a big hug, surprises me with a kiss, and tugs open the door heading back inside to settle his account.

I'm left alone at the table with the peroxide blond and the handsome, dark-haired guy with the gleaming black eyes. Actually, they don't seem to like each other very much. In fact, each one acts like the other isn't there. The attractive Spanish guy hasn't said a word.

I introduce myself to the effeminate blond, who lisps out a name I immediately forget. Then I turn to the quiet Spaniard. I offer my hand and ask his name. I can't understand what he says, so I ask him to repeat it. The name sounds like Ugo. He has to repeat it several times, because he pronounces it the Spanish way, without the H.

Before I can engage him in conversation, however, the scruffy little femm speaks up in a timid voice.

"You look like a cat lover to me," he says in a soft purr.

I'm horrified that he's right. "Yeah, well, I do have a little pal at home."

Changes

"I can tell," he says in his meek whisper. "You have empathy. Your cat can tell, and so can I."

I don't want to talk about my cat, and I don't particularly want to talk to him. "Oh, really?" I'm about to say something to Hugo across the table when the little stubbly fellow cuts me off.

"What kind of cat is it?"

"Black-and-white shorthair male."

"He's very lucky."

"Thanks."

"He's trained you well."

We laugh.

"Could I meet your cat?"

"Um, well, I live two miles..."

"I can walk with you."

Suddenly I'm bumped by someone standing beside me. I'm looking up into the round swell of a gut. It's Viking, and he's looming over me menacingly. I'm surprised to see he looks miffed. "Are we being good out here?" he barks. "What are you two talking about? Should I be jealous?"

Jealous?

The femmy blond titters. Viking bumps past me up to little Mister Peroxide and to my amazement they embrace.

I've been sitting with the jealous boyfriend.

Viking can see that I've figured it out. He leans up to me and whispers in my ear, "The last time he got jealous, he started crying. Right here at the bar. I had to take him home."

Changes

As they fall into the murmured matters of lovers and forget my existence, I move around the rickety table to the chair beside the quiet Spanish guy.

I smile.

He smiles.

I don't know it yet, but I'm about to learn that Hugo came here two years ago from Guadalajara City. He lives in the University District. He walks to Changes just like I do. In an hour I'll be suggesting that we walk home together, and we'll be walking out of the patio through the crowded bar, past guys with darts and pool cues who smile at us as though they can see right through us, as though they know what we're feeling and what we're going to do as Hugo and I head for the door out into the night.

Changes

FORCE OF NATURE

He was the last person I expected to see there.

I caught a glimpse of him over against the wall. What in the world was Jordan doing here, and why hadn't he told me he was coming? What's more, he had tears in his eyes. I could see that much from where I was sitting. Jordan, crying? He was the luckiest person I knew. What could he be crying about in public?

He was standing back away from the bar, leaning up against the coolers, next to the pull-tab machines and the line where guys stand to throw darts. I didn't notice him at first, even though I must have walked right past him. Now, sitting on the bench on the other side of the pool table, I couldn't help but see his strangely-upturned face, not acknowledging me, his former best friend, not looking at any of us, not checking out the hot guys or even paying much attention to the beer in his hand, but just staring up over our heads, like he could see the Lord coming down feet-first through the ceiling.

I watched him for a while, not obviously, of course, but pissed and puzzled that my former best friend, who hadn't talked to me since storming out of there, would show up here again, and especially in such a needy, miserable condition, shocked and worried that he could let himself go like that in a

Changes

bar, not caring what anyone thought and just breaking down in tears. He hardly moved a muscle, like a straight guy who'd wandered into the wrong bar and was fighting not to have a nervous breakdown.

I finished off the last swallow of my Long Island. Usually one is enough. Not tonight. It looked like a good time to visit the bartender. Pushing off from the bench, I negotiated my way around the end of a cocky young twink's pool cue and passed by Jordan close enough to say hello.

He didn't hear me. He didn't appear to see me at all. His attention was focused completely elsewhere. While getting my money out of my pocket to pay Earl for my drink, I looked up where Jordan was staring. A television suspended above the bar showed a helicopter rescuing two trembling small black children out of what looked like a turbulent river but was really a flooded street.

"Worst storm of the century," said Earl. The bald young bartender slid me another Long Island across the counter. "New Orleans is underwater."

That was how I first heard about it. Jordan's face was my first awareness of it. The sound of the news channel had been muted, but teletype words were streaming along the bottom of the picture. I caught the word "Katrina" and remembered the headlines about the hurricane I'd glimpsed in newspaper kiosks on my walk up to the tavern. I thought maybe boats knocked about at sea, a few resorts closed, a few cancelled airline flights.

Changes

Not this.

Not whole neighborhoods with only the roofs showing. Not people screaming and waving their arms for rescue. Not thousands drowned. I stared in disbelief as the forces of nature began to erase a legendary city.

"Hey, man, the rest of us want drinks, too," said a guy bumping me aside with his gut and stepping in front of me. I realized I'd been holding up the line. I backed away from the bar, but this time instead of returning to the pool bench, I stopped beside Jordan staring up at the television screen.

Did he notice that it was me? He must have. He didn't ask how I was or say he was sorry, or say much of anything. He clearly couldn't have cared less whether he had company or not. His beer was half-raised, approaching his mouth but not quite there. He seemed to have forgotten he was thirsty. For a couple minutes we simply stood side by side, untouched by the yelps of delight from the pool table or bursts of laughter from the end of the bar. Soon I had become like him, hypnotized by one horrifying image after another. There was only one reality – the drowning of New Orleans.

"It's so horrible I can hardly believe my eyes," I said before I realized anything was coming out of my mouth. At first I wasn't sure he'd heard me. Then he seemed to recover his senses long enough to complete the task of raising his beer to his mouth and draining it.

He mumbled something so softly I couldn't hear him, but it seemed like he was talking to me. He didn't so much as

Changes

glance in my direction, but he wiped the back of his knuckles across his eyes to smear away the wetness. A huge black woman in a sopping T-shirt, waist deep in the swirling, contaminated water, was clutching her two wide-eyed children as though they were the only things she had left in this world.

"Makes you feel like you don't have any problems," I said. "Not compared to them, I mean."

This time he heard me, all right, but when he slowly turned in my direction and acknowledged my existence, the look on his face was as harrowed as though Katrina had personally stripped him of everything he held dear. He blinked, trying to bring me into focus, trying to decide whether we even spoke the same language.

"Jordan, are you okay?"

He shook his head slowly. He wasn't okay.

A chorus of glee erupted from around the pool table, and one of the players burst into a series of triumphant leaps. Without looking at me, Jordan mumbled, "He left this morning. He's down there."

At first I wasn't sure I'd heard right. Down there where? Who was he talking about, and surely he didn't mean in ravaged Louisiana? I shot a glance in his direction, but the attention seemed to annoy him, so I turned my eyes back to the newscast and waited for him to go on, hoping I'd be able to figure out what he was talking about.

"I told him it was over last week."

Changes

Now I was truly shocked. "Are you telling me you broke up with Aaron?"

He didn't bother to answer me. "I'm the one who did it. We were together three years. What are you supposed to do when love dies? Pretend?"

What could I say to that? How could anyone be lucky enough to have Aaron Weinstein as his lover, and throw it away? I like to think that if I were ever lucky enough to find someone, I would keep the love alive. A drenched, shirtless man was comforting his sobbing wife in his arms, while helicopters whup-whup-whupped overhead.

"There are no rules when it comes to love," I said. It filled the gap. It was something I'd read somewhere once, and of course it sounded dumb as a post as soon as it came out of my mouth.

Mercifully he didn't comment. The look he gave me was enough.

"Is he trapped there?" I asked. "Is he in danger?"

"Nah, he went down there on purpose."

"You've got to be kidding."

"I went to see his mother yesterday. She lives in a retirement home. She doesn't know we've broken up yet. She told me he sent a thousand dollars to the flood relief."

Now that impressed me. An A-list gay man who had values beyond expensive clothes, flashy car, exclusive parties, who had compassion... "What a guy." I was scrambling for an explanation. "Is he from New Orleans?"

Changes

He didn't hear my question. "But that wasn't enough. Not for him. Money, he can afford to give money. So his mom says he stayed up all night making the right phone calls and this morning he jumped on a plane and now he's down there volunteering."

"I am so impressed."

"He'll be a volunteer emergency doctor. His mom says he'll be working in a football stadium full of evacuees."

Struggle as I might, I couldn't make it all add up. "Aaron is such an awesome guy, he sounds too good to be true," I fumbled. "I mean, it sounds like you're telling me you just said goodbye to the perfect partner. I don't understand. The way you talk about him, you still love him."

Though he seemed to be looking up at the screen, I felt he was no longer really seeing it.

"I feel nothing," he said with sad finality.

The idea that someone could throw away the very thing I most wanted gnawed at me. I couldn't let it go.

"What was the problem? Was he boring?"

The ghost of a smile touched his lips. "Never. Intelligent as hell. Always reading."

"Is he some kind of religious nut?"

"He's the kindest and most moral man I ever met."

My questions were getting me nowhere, and I was losing patience. "Then what could possibly make you leave Aaron Weinstein? A guy who'd give a thousand dollars to flood relief and then fly down there to volunteer?"

Changes

He seemed to be trying to find the words somewhere in his mouth, to force them to come out of his lips and make sense, when the front door of the bar creaked open with that unmistakable sound that all night long would cause idle eyes to turn in that direction.

In walked a muscular Latino god straight out of a porn movie. He was someone we'd never seen before, head like a Roman bust, bare shoulders like mahogany banister knobs. His tanktop wasn't meant to hide much, and didn't. He walked up to Jordan with a big grin and said, *"Hola, papi chulo."* Then he put his arms around his neck, took his head in his hands like a coconut, and drilled his tongue into him.

The bar stood still. We could all feel it.

While the young hottie draped his lovely muscles all over him, Jordan turned in my direction and looked right through me. He had the eyes of a man who has just made a decision that has ripped through his life and gutted it. I was looking at the victim of a force of nature.

His young friend never once glanced at the television screen. Instead he put his arm around Jordan's waist and guided him out of the tavern, while water and wind did their best to blow a city off the face of the earth.

Changes

KISS OF THE POOL SHARK

We were all admiring him. There was a lot to admire.

The guy must have been in his late thirties, a scruffy blond with a hairline just starting to recede, a brown stubble of several days' growth, and penetrating ice-blue eyes with slightly reddened whites. His body was still lean and perfectly distributed but thicker and toughened with age. His tanktop fit him like a glove, which he knew. Every turn, every line-up of cue and balls seemed like a photo shoot as he positioned himself on the green felt in various sprawls and crouches with the agility of a young boy, stretching out boldly across the table to reach for impossible shots.

"Mmm, isn't he a beauty?" sighed Brad beside me. I didn't have to ask who he meant. It was almost a joke, the way we were all so spellbound. You had to concentrate to force yourself to look away from him. "Makes me wish for just a minute that I wasn't married."

Brad was clearly bored, but being a good sport. He was missing dinner at home with his lover, not to mention a segment of the PBS history of American musicals, followed by his favorite armchair reading of Victorian biographies. His diet Coke was resting on his unconcealed paunch, which he presented to the world as a welcoming front porch. His thick

Changes

white beard threatened to dunk inside the glass and stir the ice cubes. The dear man was constantly inviting me to dinner, and tonight I'd accepted, persuading him to drive up to Changes for the Tuesday night special of $1.50 burger-and-fries.

We were sitting on the pool bench against the far wall, watching the youngest of the local boys compete. Boyish, meaty Kenny with the turned-up polo shirt collar was taking on the afternoon winner. One by one, the sexy pool shark had cleaned up every challenger. Now it was Kenny's turn, and in this David-and-Goliath match we were Kenny's cheering section and support group.

Brad turned to the tall, skinny boy standing beside him, anxiously fingering his cue, the next in line to be beaten. "Who is that guy?" Brad pointed at the one we were all trying not to ogle.

"That's Daryl," he said. "Daryl's the best. He used to come here all the time."

As though right on cue, Daryl came striding around the pool table. "You boys talking about me?"

Without waiting for an answer, he turned his back, raised his cue, aimed, and started backing straight toward me. Suddenly I found myself right behind him and totally in the way. I veered impulsively in the other direction.

A terrible wet shattering exploded uncomfortably close by. It brought the bar to a hush. I looked where I'd just set my drink, and it wasn't there anymore. I glanced at the floor.

Changes

Something wet was seeping around the edge of the bench, making a pool around a piece of broken glass.

I got a round of applause. I was too embarrassed to even glance in Daryl's direction. Brad was jumping to his feet to help me set things right, but I waved him back.

"I'll get a rag," I mumbled, and hurried around to the bartender's station. I had it all quickly mopped up and the sharp bits of glass off the floor. I could see Brad was red-cheeked from laughing.

I tried to see the humor in it.

I couldn't.

Kenny has always been a pleasure to watch, with his boy next door freckles, youthful plumpness and tight shirts, and we cheered him on. But he was no match for the shark. The guy was casual about his shots, almost reckless. We would gasp as he pocketed them, one by one. Kenny gave him a good run for his money, but his struggle was brief and ended pocket-pocket-pocket.

Kenny smiled his brave, good sport smile and held out the loser's hand to be shaken. Instead Daryl kissed him.

Did I mention that Brad had bought me another drink and that I was halfway through it? I must have been plowed to do what I did next, or else just not aware of how loudly I was talking. "Wow," I said, in open admiration of the kiss, "I'm going to take up pool."

The guys around the pool table laughed.

I did not expect Daryl to turn and look at me.

Changes

No one expected him to walk up to me, take my cheeks in both his callused paws, and give me a deep-throated, breathless kiss. Least of all me. When he finally pulled his mouth away from mine, I had to suck air in desperately. Good thing I did, because he promptly grabbed me by the chin, pulled me toward him, and kissed me again, longer and deeper.

And again.

When he finally let me go, I was so light-headed I nearly slid off the pool bench. My bones had turned to Jell-O.

"I'm sick of pool," said Daryl. "Let's go. I'll be right back. I'm just closing out my card."

Luck was luck, but this was ridiculous. I stood there in shock, reeling from the kisses, slowly regaining my sense of appropriate behavior. Brad was smiling at me. I could see he was itching to go.

"Looks like you're taken care of, big boy."

"What am I doing right?"

"Enjoy it. Think I'm going to head home to my honey."

"Needless to say, I'll be sticking around," I said with a smile. "Thanks for dinner. Goodnight. Um, are you sure you can find your car? You remember last time."

Brad scowled. "Yes, I remember last time, thank you very much. I like to think I learn from my mistakes. I remember perfectly well where I parked, and I'll see you tomorrow at work, I hope."

Changes

I watched him leave.

I remember the bar shifting direction slightly. Not until then did I realize I'd had a little more to drink than I thought.

I had to back up against a stool to keep my balance. Unfortunately, the stool was occupied. Luckily, none of his drink spilled on him. The guy let me know what he thought of my bad manners but I don't remember what he said because Daryl grabbed my hand and drew me after him down the length of the bar and out the door into the night.

I think we just went around the corner, but I don't remember doing it. I remember where we ended up was on a neighborhood curb, half a block away from the streetlamp in the shadows under some trees, and I was backed up against his parked car.

One minute he's nibbling at my neck, the next minute he drops in a dead collapse onto the parking strip.

I can hardly believe my eyes. What a nightmare. I panic. Oh, my God. He's hyperventilating. It's a drug overdose. It's heart failure.

His arms were floppy and useless. His legs no longer seemed to work. I tried to haul him up onto his feet. Unconscious people weigh much more than you think. I could hardly budge him. My little romantic miracle had gone way, way bad. I was about to be implicated in a drug death.

He opened his eyes and struggled up off the grass onto one knee.

"Are you okay?"

Changes

"Sure, sure, it's no big deal."

With my eyes bulging, heart hammering, I would have laughed at his assessment but I was too shook up to be ironic. I helped him the rest of the way up. He held onto me, and he whispered, "Listen, I can't do this."

A few shakes went through him. I remember wrapping my arms around him trying to keep him balanced on his feet as tremors rattled through his body. "Sorry," he said. "You're really sexy and I want to mess around with you, but I can't."

"Maybe some other time," I said, not getting it.

He almost didn't go on, but then was drunk enough to admit, "I've got a partner. Sorry. I should never have kissed you like that."

Then he threw up.

I got him turned around just in time, and held onto him while he tossed up his dinner and who knows what else, that hunky body bucking in my arms, fortunately keeping his spewing mouth aimed away from us, so that when only the dry heaves were left we both emerged relatively free of debris.

"Thanks," he mumbled. "I'd give you another kiss, but I don't think you'd appreciate it."

He swung open the driver's door.

"So, lemme explain something. My boyfriend isn't doing so well." The way he said it, I knew what he was talking about. "He's starting to get sick a lot."

"I'm sorry," I said. I meant it. What else can you say?

Changes

"He doesn't look as good as he used to." His voice shook a little. He slid into the driver's seat, and slammed the door shut. The window purred down. "I mean, I still love him. But, well, I'm positive, too. I've got what he's got, he's just got it worse. And it's killing him. It's hard to watch, man. Hard to see him going downhill, know what I mean? Because I'm next. What's happening to him is going to happen to me. It's got to the point where I can't have sex with him anymore. I'm not turned on anymore. Because I can see that he's dying. Because it depresses me, and it makes me scared."

He started the engine. "Sorry, man. You're a sweet guy."

I watched him drive away.

Shoving my hands in my pockets, avoiding the mess on the ground, I turned back toward Changes to start out on the long walk home. Then I happened to glance across the street and noticed Brad standing on the corner, hands on his hips, scowling in all directions. I laughed, waited for a break in the traffic, and darted across the street.

His face lit up when he saw me. "Thank God. I can't find it anywhere. I've been wandering for blocks. Where the hell did I park it?"

"Come on, I think it's down this way."

PEACEMAKER

I looked up and there he was beside me, searching through the jar of darts for the good ones.

I was leaning against the back wall of the bar, between the pull-tab machines and the coat rack, and didn't realize the dart jar was beside me on one of the coolers. He had a likeable, healthy, refreshing look, like he'd been a jock back in high school and never lost that image, all shoulder bones and jutting chin, baseball cap on backwards, a fuzzy little soul patch under his lower lip.

Something clicked, and I suddenly knew for certain that I'd seen him somewhere before. I just couldn't remember exactly where.

After ten minutes of indecision, I was about to force myself to do the right thing and get up the nerve to speak to him when he turned away with his three selected missiles, put some quarters in the electronic dartboard, and started playing against himself. I watched him. He must have been in his early thirties, lean face and lean body, carrying himself with confidence, like every muscle knew exactly what to do. He wore a faded red baseball jersey with a frayed collar and the sleeves pushed up.

He was the classic guy next door.

Changes

I cracked up watching him. He made all kinds of faces while he threw the darts, grins and grimaces and winces and sucks, as though he were really two guys determined to beat each other. He appeared to be totally unself-conscious, like he was in the tavern alone, as though no one else's opinion mattered in the slightest. Since he seemed to be enjoying himself, I was surprised when the machine beeped for more quarters to see him shrug and turn back to the wall beside me.

"I won," he said glibly, taking time for a swallow.

"Congratulations."

"Or I lost. Depending on which one I was." He gave me an assessing look, like he was trying to guess my nationality. "You play darts?"

"I've been known to throw a dart or two," I said. "Tell me, it's driving me crazy. Why do you look so familiar?"

He smiled. "Lots of people ask me that." He developed a sudden thirst, sucked up enough beer to lower the level in his glass by a couple inches, and as he slurped it down he gave me an appraising look with eyes like razors. "Were you here the night of the fight?"

That got my attention. "Were you here, too?"

That kind of thing didn't happen at Changes. It was packed that Tuesday, the dollar beers were flying, everybody smelled like hamburgers, the spirits were high. Earl was nudging and bumping his way through the crowd, juggling platters of steaming hot burgers and fries which he delivered straight from the grill with the grace of a ballerina.

Changes

Some guys had been there for quite some time, downing those dollar beers, and among them had been a familiar couple, Buck and Mitchell, two attractive professional men in their thirties who had been partners for six months. Buck was gregarious, Mitchell was gorgeous, and though both of them were usually well-mannered, they could be loud and festive at the right alcoholic levels.

Those levels had been reached that night.

I can remember watching them over on the far bench all night. Every time Mitchell wandered away to talk with another guy, Buck would bellow, "Girl!" and expect him to return. Mitchell began to ignore him. Buck yelled louder. Mitchell was talking at length about his favorite topic, his workout, complaining that he'd been gaining weight. Buck denied it, and proudly hauled up Mitchell's shirt to prove it, allowing us all to admire his lover's heartbreakingly attractive torso. Mitchell endured it. Clearly it wasn't the first time.

We were all smiling at Buck, hating him and jealous and hoping he'd show us more of Mitchell's body when Colby stepped up to the bar beside me and Shawn asked him what he wanted to drink. For one split second, I glanced away from them to greet Colby, so I missed what actually triggered it. Mitchell and Buck were eating by then, both had plates of burgers and fries, at least that's what I seem to remember, although what I really remember, of course, were the shouts when they both jumped to their feet, hurling their food at each

Changes

other, clattering plates, mayo on the chest, lettuce on the pool table, buns and patties and fries all over the place.

Both drinks got knocked over across the bench. A stool went down. Neither of them even seemed to notice. They were both furious with each other, shouting and accusing and denying in a blaze of jealousy and hurt feelings, a hullabaloo about who didn't really love the other, as though food and beer and stools didn't matter, shoving each other with outstretched arms, yelling in each other's faces.

Their nasty little squabble was becoming nastier by the minute. People were backing away. Shawn shouted something sensible at them, with no response, and the young bartender was nervously hurrying around from behind the bar, clearly freaked out but determined to intervene. He never got there.

Someone else got there first.

Suddenly one of their friends shoved his way in between them, pushed them apart, and managed to shout both of them to their senses. The peacemaker seemed to be one of their pals. His baseball cap hid most of his face. He got right in there and pulled them apart. Once they were separated and the music was turned up, the bar went back to enjoying itself, buzzing over the little melodrama and laughing with relief that it was over.

The entire episode lasted less than two minutes. It was talked about for weeks.

"You were here, too, huh?" I said. "That was something else, wasn't it? Did you ever hear what was it that got those

Changes

guys going? We just figured it was some kind of lovers' quarrel."

"You could call it that," he said.

"So that must be why you look familiar. I must have seen you there."

He was no longer looking me in the eye. "I was the one who broke up the fight."

"That was *you?*" I took another look at him, and recognized him with a laugh. "Oh, my God. Of course." I tried to picture his face that night, but now all I could remember for sure was his baseball cap.

"My name's Trent," he said, shaking my hand. "I was stupid enough to try to help them."

"Stupid?" That was unexpected. "What makes you say that? Blessed are the peacemakers, I thought."

"Damned are the peacemakers."

That surprised me. "Were they your buddies?"

"They were friends of friends. I liked them both. They were both cute, fun to hang out with. I talked to them separately after it happened, heard them out. Convinced both of them to come to my house, to spill it out in front of each other, figure out what went wrong."

"What a good guy," I had to comment. "And? Did you succeed?"

He smiled at me, an odd smile. It was more sad than happy. "Depends on what you mean by succeed. As for getting them back together, no, it was a disaster. Buck stormed out. Mitchell ended up spending the night at my place, crying his heart out, a complete wreck."

"Spent the night, huh?" I gave him an inquiring look. "On the sofa?"

He smiled tightly. "I put a row of pillows between us."

I raised an eyebrow.

Trent shrugged. "Okay, he pushed away the pillows. Guys are just animals, face it. We didn't fight it very hard. So I totally fucked up and caused the exact opposite of what I was trying to do." He tipped his beer into his mouth, while his eyes remained fixed on some place in the past. "For three days Mitchell stayed at my place, before Buck would let him back in the house. Those days were heaven. I didn't go to work. We didn't get dressed. We could hardly get out of bed."

He took a long drink. I watched his Adam's apple bobbing.

"Then he and Buck patched it up. It was unexpected. It was a shock, actually. I was in deeper than I thought. I was lost without him. We tried to leave it behind. We couldn't. We'd developed a taste for each other. Now we're supposed to turn it off? Fuck that."

He finished his beer, and put the empty bottle on the shelf behind him. "For one sweet week after another we lied. We came up with a million excuses for blind, loud, good-natured Buck. We tricked him. We fucked with his mind. I watched him turn insecure, suspicious, paranoid. Did we stop, when we saw what it was doing to him? No, we just kept on lying, right to his face, both of us nearly insane with lust. When lust gets in your brain, you don't feel guilty, you just go after what you want. Poor Buck was a wreck. Finally Mitchell couldn't stand it anymore. He told Buck their relationship was over, and that he was moving in with me."

The story stopped. Trent studied the dartboard, as though the numbers had arranged themselves differently than usual. Maybe he was done, maybe he was just pausing, I couldn't tell.

"I can't believe I'm telling you all this," he said at last.

I was tongue-tied, but mumbled something.

He tapped a cigarette out of a package, and dropped the cigarette. He tapped out another. His hands were shaking.

"Guess I needed to tell somebody," he conceded, lighting it and sucking on the end of it like he was trying to get back his past. "Don't worry, Mitchell and I didn't last for long." He took another drag, deciding how much to tell me. "After three effing days of the best sex Mitchell or I ever had in our lives, he went back to Buck. Why? Who the fuck knows? He said he felt too guilty, that he'd made a commitment, that he had to do the right thing. He said he couldn't live without his self-respect, crap like that."

Again the story seemed to stop. Or maybe Trent was getting choked up, just waiting till his emotions were under control. He finished up the cigarette hungrily, like he needed smoke to survive.

Changes

"Well," I offered, "I admire him for having some kind of principles."

"Yeah, maybe," he said. "Except now we're lovers in secret."

My look of surprise made him laugh.

"Mitchell's honor lasted two days. Then there's a knock on my door at seven in the morning, and all of a sudden, there he is pulling off his jogging shorts, his honor doesn't matter so much. What matters is Mitchell just had a fight with Buck, and so he's yanking off my clothes and pushing me back on the bed. That's what matters."

He fumbled another cigarette out of the pack, dropping the pack and spilling the other cigarettes out over the floor. His hand shook as he lit it. "Who cares about the rest? What matters is I've got my man back." I couldn't tell if he was laughing or choking on sobs that wouldn't come out. "I've got Mitchell back for an hour here, a couple hours there. Maybe I get him back for an afternoon on the weekend."

He took a long drag, and held it in as long as he could..

"Now we just lie to everybody. Now we're always sneaking, he's always looking at his watch, and we jump when the phone rings. Look at me now – what do you see? A guy getting drunk in a bar who's not with the guy he loves. Why not? Because the man I love is in bed with Buck."

His lips shaped the name with sheer contempt.

"Buck, Buck, Buck. Well, I've got the advantage. I know all about Buck, but Buck doesn't know about me. Hah!

Changes

I'm just waiting for my next turn with Mitchell, when he's going to tell me how much he needs me and misses me, and how much better I make love."

"And you believe him?"

"Of course." Trent's eyes were dark with unexpressed misery, but he forced them to look confident. "Why would he lie to me? I'm the one he loves. Come on, play a game of darts with me. I can only pretend to be two different people for so long."

"If you need someone to beat you, I'm the guy."

"We'll see about that." He grinned awkwardly, the grimace of a brave soldier trying to show that amputation doesn't hurt.

I reached in and fished three darts out of the bowl.

"The only thing is," he added, "if my phone rings and it's Mitchell, I might have to go. That's the one condition." He drained the last of his beer and stepped forward, arranging his feet behind the throw-line. "Shitty, huh? Try to save a guy's marriage, and you end up becoming his mistress. Oh, well." He aimed. "It isn't easy for him, either. We can't be choosy. We have to take what we can get."

Changes

THE SOURCE OF ALL PAIN

Actually, I thought Craig didn't like me. Imagine my surprise last night when he warmly invited me over to meet his friends.

I had spotted him first from across the bar, but only because I thought he was an attractive guy. Saturdays aren't the best nights at Changes, and he was the one standout there. I ordered my drink and looked again. This time I thought he looked familiar. Then I realized who he was, a fellow I'd met back in August, but who tonight was sporting a whole new look. A dapper little black fringe beard now outlined his lips and jaw.

He was sitting over on the other side of the pool table, on that inaccessible bench between the dartboard and the cue rack. At first he appeared to be alone. He saw me looking at him and waved. Since a pool game was in progress I made no attempt to approach him. I waved back. Then, just because I felt like throwing out a compliment, I used my hand to pantomime a beard around my own mouth and jaw, to show that I'd noticed his new facial adornment, and then gave a thumb's up to show that I thought it looked hot.

That's when his two friends emerged from the patio doorway, two guys in their forties in button-down shirts. They

Changes

appeared to find my little mime so amusing they immediately began making hand motions in return that were a jumble of hula moves, Boy Scout code and sign language, while giving me big toothy smiles.

Annoyed, I pretended not to notice.

A few minutes later Craig got up, waited for the little lesbian in front of him to make her pool shot, and then approached me.

"Hey, there. Nice to see ya." No hugs, no touches. He always greets me the same way. "I'm sorry, but I forget your name."

"You'll remember it someday, Craig." I smiled as I shook his hand. I told him my name again, even though I could tell he instantly forgot it. That should have been my clue, right there. He wasn't asking my name to remember it, in the first place.

Although Craig's words could leave a chill in the air, his body language tended to have the opposite effect. Though he wasn't exactly a lust object, he was a reasonable-looking guy who was still gut-free and could be quite attractive when he laughed. He was trim enough and healthy-looking, maybe in his early thirties, with black hair worn short and neat. He might have passed for a comfortable young accountant, but sad, troubled eyes gave it away. They were black, shiny pits, clear evidence that he'd been knocked around in life, and hadn't always won. While Craig's words warned you to keep your distance, his body stood slightly too close and begged to

Changes

be touched, like someone tempting a dog with a forbidden treat and ready to slap his nose if he goes for it.

"Come on over, and meet my friends," he said.

Instantly I concluded that his friends had put him up to approaching me. "Sure," I said. "I'll meet your friends." I saw no reason not to, although the way those friends were smiling at me made me uncomfortable.

The little lesbian was preparing to make a difficult shot, and taking her time to get it just right. She completely blocked all access to the bench. Craig took a step backward to get out of her way. His butt bumped up against my crotch. He immediately turned around and pressed his hand up against my chest as though preventing me from getting poked by her pool cue.

Funny behavior. I can tell he likes me, but he's always keeping his distance. That awkward bump, and the response it got, reminds me of the hot Tuesday afternoon back in August when we first met, a troubled meeting at best, on that very same bench over there beyond the pool table that we are now waiting to approach.

My bright, literate friend Brad and I had driven up from the bookstore. The sun was out, boys were out, life was good. After inhaling our cheeseburgers and beers and enjoying the parade of young pool players, Brad had gone off to the men's room, ostensibly to relieve himself but probably just as much to make sure there were no cheeseburger crumbs or mustard in his fluffy white beard.

Changes

At that moment, as I sat on the pool bench by myself nursing the last of my beer, Craig appeared from the patio for the first time and promptly sat down right beside me on the bench, taking Brad's place without realizing it, smiling to himself and at peace in his own world, a slightly-tipsy sadder-but-wiser guy with stubbly cheeks in a buttoned-down pin-striped shirt with the sleeves rolled up to the elbows and the buttons at the top and bottom undone.

When Brad returned, he simply plopped himself down with a knowing smile on the other side of the attractive stranger, who was surprised to find himself suddenly sitting in the middle of two friends.

"Did I just barge in between you two?" He tried to jump up, but Brad stiff-armed him right back down onto the bench.

"You're right where you belong," said Brad. "Cute men are always welcome on this bench."

"But now I'm in your way."

"It's physically impossible for an attractive man to be in the way," said Brad. "It defies the laws of physics. Besides, there's going to be plenty of room soon because there's a young whippersnapper here who needs to be taught a lesson in how to play pool."

A tall toothpick of a boy, collar up, hair spiked, who was leaning up against wall beside him, grinned while giving the nose of his cue a good rub in blue chalk. "Think you can whup me, Gramps?"

Changes

"Gramps?" Brad bounced to his feet and selected his cue, giving me a knowing nod that he was doing it for my benefit. He was leaving Craig all to me.

"I haven't been out in a long time," said Craig. "Way too long." He slurred his words just slightly. "Well, I'm having a good time tonight. This shirt is going to come off real soon."

"Well, I'm definitely looking forward to that," I said obligingly.

I couldn't tell how drunk he was. His thigh came to rest against mine. "Can you tell that I'm forty-one?"

"You've got to be kidding."

"My birthday is tomorrow. Forty-one. Too young to commit suicide, don't you think? So I've decided to turn over a new leaf. To give up all my bad habits and bad thoughts. To go back to grad school. I've already put in a year of Forestry, and I'm going back to work on my degree, right back where I left off when I decided to explore the wonderful world of chemicals." He gave me a sad smile. "I've explored just about every chemical known to man. It's been quite a sad journey. I wouldn't have told you all that if I hadn't had too many beers. Are you a Buddhist?"

I was taken aback by the abrupt transition. "Funny you should ask. I'm not really anything, but if I were, I'd be a Buddhist."

"I'm a Buddhist. And a vegetarian. I don't watch television. I don't drive a car. I'm a believer in careful living.

Changes

But no matter how carefully you live your life, you can never be careful enough."

He rose to his feet, swept up in his own ardor. "Being human means fucking up. It means you're never careful enough." His thigh was banging against my knee. "Because no matter how hard you try, you can't stop causing pain."

That was where I made my mistake. Thinking that my outthrust foot was blocking him from getting closer, I turned my shoe sideways.

"Chill," he said sternly.

At first I thought he wasn't talking to me. Then I tried to back my foot away from him.

"Chill out," he said, as though dealing with a recalcitrant child. "I mean it, just chill."

That moment changed everything. His shirt didn't come off. He got up and played pool, and I disappeared from his horizon. Brad and I said goodbye to him when we left. He didn't seem to hear us. But just as we turned to walk out, he tugged at my arm. "Do you have a card? You and I have unfinished business. We need to talk."

I gave him my card. I never heard from him again.

I'd almost forgotten about Craig when he appeared before me one morning a month later, half-protected by a friend's dripping umbrella, in the downpouring rain. We were among the five thousand gathered on the grassy, wet lawns of Volunteer Park for the Seattle AIDS Walk. The crowd was just beginning to move, spilling down the hill which quickly

Changes

became a brown slope of mud, when our umbrellas bumped into each other. We were both drenched, anyway. There was no way to stay dry.

"Hey, there," I said. "Nice to bump into you."

He beamed and came so close the spokes of his umbrella got tangled in mine.

We laughed, and then he fumbled out the same greeting he seemed to always have for me. "I'm sorry, I don't remember your name."

I told him. The crowd bumped him one way, my friends went the other.

Since then, I'd seen him at Changes several times, and he was always unpredictable. Sometimes he seemed oblivious to my existence. Sometimes he seemed hyper-aware of every breath I took.

The last time I saw him our eyes locked the minute I walked in the door. Instead of ordering a drink, I went straight up to him, and his reception had been warmer than ever before. But when I left to order my drink and came back, it was like the unfriendly twin had taken his place. He wanted nothing to do with me. He excused himself and went elsewhere.

Now, here he was again on this slow Saturday night, warmly escorting me over to meet his friends, sitting down with his pals on one side, me on the other. Suddenly the chill comes over him again.

Changes

"Something about your life is interesting," he says, poking me in the chest with his finger. "What is it? Didn't you write a book or something?"

I admit that I have. That seems to do it. The topic changes. He gets up and sits on the other side of his friends, as far away from me as he can get.

Those were the last words we said to each other. I talked with one of his friends until they decided to leave. All three of them got up and waited for an appropriate break in the pool table action. Craig would have walked right past me, but I reached out and caught his arm.

"Nice to see you again, Craig," I said, slowing him down just a moment in his exit.

"Yeah, nice to see you, too," he said, and walked on. Thinking they'd left, I abandoned the lonely bench and went back to the metal shelf over the coolers. From there I could watch blushing Kenny and the other young regulars play darts. But though Craig's two friends were on their way out the tavern door, Craig was remaining behind at the bar, straddling the stool beside the cash register waiting to settle his drinking tab.

There he was, a few steps away, impatient for Shawn to finish with the guys in front of him. It was my chance, and I took it. I slipped onto the stool beside him and said, "Craig, why is it I always feel like I've offended you?"

That got his attention. "You feel what?"

Changes

"Like I bug you. Like you're suspicious of me. I'm guilty of something in your book. What is it?"

He laughs in embarrassment. "Is it that obvious?"

At least he's acknowledging that it's real. "Why do you have a grudge against me?"

"Sorry. It's so fucked of me. It's not your fault. It's me. Well, it's embarrassing."

He might have told me right then, except that Shawn presented him with a receipt to sign and his bank card. When he turned back to me, Greg asked, "Do you know much about Buddhism?"

"Oh, a micro-tad."

"Well, one of the key beliefs is that the source of all pain is desire. Wanting is what makes us hurt. Wanting causes people to suffer."

"That much I've heard."

"Well, I haven't exactly led a perfect life. I've made a few mistakes, you could say. I know all about desire. I was killing myself with desire. Buddhism saved me. Now when I feel desire, yes, I feel it, but I let it go past me. I know where desire can lead. I can't go there anymore. And, well, you fill me with desire."

"I like that."

"Too much. I could never keep my center around someone like you. And so I fight you. I push you away. I'm through with wanting. That's part of my past. From now on, I'm accepting. I'm surrendering. I'm letting go. When I meet someone who fills me with wanting, with the poison of discontent, I make myself stay away. No more wanting for me. Because wanting gets inside you. Wanting can eat your soul."

He took my head in both his hands and kissed me. It was a sweet kiss, the kiss he really wanted to give me. It didn't last long. He snapped out of it, and started to push me out of the way, so he could hurry unimpeded toward the door. The look on his face was pure unhappiness.

"Wait, Craig" I said. Craig!"

"You're hurting me, man."

"I can see that…"

"I'm in pain just looking at you. I do not want to ache for you. Stay away from me."

"Craig, it's you. You're turning it into pain. You're making pain for yourself out of trying to avoid pain."

I would have laughed away his rigorous precautions to show him that we could get past it, but he was too far down the length of the bar to hear me.

Changes

DIVIDED ATTENTION

She was clearly in the wrong bar, and too caught up in her phone conversation to realize it.

"That's exactly what I told him but he wasn't listening, no, not him, he never listens, he's too good for that, he knows better, and ya know what, he's got shit for brains…"

Admittedly the woman was annoying.

Why she wandered in off the street was anyone's guess. Her baby blue pedal-pushers were way too tight on her skinny shanks, and between them and the flimsy shoes she was trying to balance on, she waddled into the bar like some drag queen sadly out of practice. The tight white denim jacket and her straggly, over-sprayed blond hair were more suited to one of the straight bars up the street, so her whole appearance there, jabbering into her cell phone as she plopped herself down on a bar stool, was an accident, the wrong woman at the wrong place at the wrong time.

Which was no reason to yell at her.

I don't remember exactly what the guy next to her said. Something like "Shut the fuck up." Along those lines. He roared the words right in her ear and totally freaked her, not so

Changes

much by what he said as by the sheer loudness. She was so startled that she dropped the damned thing. The clatter when it hit the floor sounded louder than it should have, and got more attention than it deserved.

That kind of thing doesn't happen at Changes. Conversations skidded to a halt. Everyone was suddenly listening to every word. Standing back against the wall behind them, I didn't know whether to bolt or interfere. It happened so fast no one knew exactly what to do.

"Hey, who do you think you are?" she snapped.

Earl the bartender came striding right over, the man in charge as always. "Do we have a problem here?"

She was crouching down between the bar stools, picking up her cell-phone out of the pull-tabs littering the floor in piles like the crisp little bodies of dead insects.

"We sure do have a problem," she barked out to Earl and all of us witnesses, as though we'd back her up. "This guy is out of his mind." Then into her cell phone she says, "This guy here is giving me shit…"

That was all the farther she got.

"Get that thing away from me," said the angry man next to her. It was a bellow, and shut her up fast. Civilized people don't talk that loud in close quarters.

"Hey, buddy, keep your voice down," said Earl. Nobody else made a peep.

That Monday night there were only about a dozen of us there, but I think most of us would have agreed that the loud, disagreeable woman had violated any common sense of proper boundaries.

Still, that didn't give anyone the right to shout at her.

"What the hell is your problem?" she snapped, wavering on her feet. She looked around for a support group she seemed to find missing, because her countenance fell. "Is that how you treat people here?"

"You, too, lady," said Earl. "What are you doing in a gay bar?"

She looked at him blankly. Then she shouted into her cell phone, "They're all fags in this place!" and lurched out the front door.

It took one split second for the place to recover itself. Amid an outburst of laughter and cries of "Wrong bar, sweetheart," her exit was followed by whistles of derision, applause, and a flurry of obscene one-liners released by the now vocal gay crowd that a moment before had been stricken silent with urban panic. Hoots and clapping and suddenly-bold derogatory comments whisked her on her way.

Only the guy who had yelled at her had nothing more to contribute. Clearly he didn't find the situation amusing. Since we'd witnessed a sample of his anger, no one felt like bringing out more of it.

Five minutes later, their wit exhausted, everyone seemed to forget the incident and the man, too.

I took another sip of my Long Island. The stool next to the angry man was available. It took me another couple sips to get up my nerve. Then I cautiously stepped away from the wall and slid onto the seat, like a nervous cowboy lowering himself down onto a bronco known to buck.

He froze. I could feel the tension in his body all the way over on the next stool.

Fortunately Earl came strolling down the bar toward us, wiping up a spill with one hand, picking up a couple empty glasses with the other. "What do you think of my decorations?" he asked, interrupting the silence that had gripped us. "Don't they look great? This place is going totally Halloween for the whole month. I love it. It's my favorite time of year. Fuck Christmas. I've got more spiderwebs and bones coming, and I've got a great idea for that back wall." He was effervescing with excitement, looking as hunky as ever in that tight black T-shirt. "Gay people love Halloween. It's our holiday. We're all in drag. That's what life's all about, really, isn't it? Drag."

Earl drifts away to help other customers. I can tell the guy next to me has been listening to us. Still, he says nothing. I try not to watch him, try not to make him feel stared at, but basically he's just working on his beer and not looking at anyone. So when he says through clenched teeth, "I hate those things," at first I'm not even sure he's talking to me.

The guy's having a rough night, so he's not looking his best. It's been a while since he shaved, or maybe changed his shirt. His hair looks more like it was shoved in the right direction than combed. I'd call him lean, except he had an undernourished quality that makes him look scrawny. He was a big city survivor, slumped over on his elbows, staring into his glass of beer like it was due to change into a crystal ball any minute.

He looked at me and tried to make his mouth smile, but it was mostly determination I saw in the tight line of his lips and very little humor. I felt like I'd missed a line. "Did you say something to me?"

That really cracked him up. "Shocking, isn't it? Nobody talks to anybody anymore. Ever notice that?" Those sad eyes of his poked right into mine, diving in way too deep. I flinched, and looked away. "Everybody's in their own little world these days, zoned into their headsets, talking into their cell phones. Nobody wants to just look you in the eye and talk to you face-to-face."

"I know what you mean," I said sincerely.

He gave me a look of relief, of quiet appreciation. "You ever hear of divided attention?"

I wasn't sure what he was talking about.

"That's what those damned things are causing. It's a killer. Stress and divided attention will destroy us all." I couldn't tell what he was drinking, but he knocked off another one. "That's the problem in a nutshell, divided attention. Everyone thinks they can get away with using only half a brain. Isn't that ripe? What a civilization. Use as little brain as possible. Everyone thinks they're so clever and worldly they've got half a brain to spare, why not use it to zone out, enjoy a little music or learn a foreign language or talk dirty with your boyfriend. Drive with half a brain, chat with half. Walk with half, talk with half. The thing about divided attention, everyone thinks they can do it."

He looked me straight in the eye.

"Don't you?" His eyes were so aggressive there was nowhere to hide. "Tell the truth. You think you can get away with it. You think you can do two things at once, and no one will know the difference. But if anybody else tries it, you can spot it a mile away."

I hated to admit he was right. "You talk like somebody who knows all about it. Did you ever have a phone?"

His mouth popped open in a tiny circle, as though I'd just stuck a knife into his gut.

"Sure, I had one once," he admitted slowly and quietly. "I'm just like everybody else. I wanted to get my calls wherever I happened to be. I wanted to be always in touch. And I was." He was looking back into memories now. "I was a popular guy. I was never far away from that thing. My friends could always reach me."

He made a funny sound in his throat. It was trying to be a laugh, but it sounded more like a sob. "It's a killer, I'm telling you, divided attention. You think you know what life is going to throw at you. But sometimes you're wrong. Most of the time you can do two things at once, but every once in a while you can't. And sometimes it changes everything. Do you hear what I'm saying? There's no going back. I'm telling you because I know, because I fucked up, talking to one of my buddies. About a football game where I lost five bucks."

Something was wrong with his throat. The words were getting caught in it. He was having a hard time getting them out. At first I thought he wasn't going to tell me anymore. I didn't think he could.

"Man, you never know when you're going to do something you'll regret for the rest of your life." His lip muscles were trembling. It's not easy to watch someone experiencing that much sadness. I had to look away. "Once it's done, it's done. There's no going back. There's no making things better. Once you fuck things up, they're fucked up for good. It's over in a second. You slam on the brakes, but it's too late. You can feel sorry as hell, you can talk to God all you want to, but it doesn't matter. You did it. And you're gonna know you did it for the rest of your life."

He slid backward off his stool.

"Enough for one night." He stuffed his arms into the sleeves of his jacket. "I'm heading home. I go to bed early now. I like being unconscious." He slid a couple bills out of his pocket, and left them on the bar. He wouldn't look me in the eye. I'd heard his confession.

"It's a good night for a walk," he said, raising the back collar of his jacket. "I don't drive anymore."

Changes

LOGICAL GROUNDS FOR HOPE

He looked like a fraternity boy who refused to grow up. He must have been pushing thirty. He still had that neat, reasonably-short, freshly brushed hair with the tidy neckline, the conservative polo shirt, the odor of a little too much deodorant going nervously sour. I noticed him loitering near me by the dartboard, hands shoved into his front pockets, rocking back and forth from one foot to the other, fiercely determined to look casual. He had a classically handsome face of the Johnny Depp school, an aristocratic head somewhat mismatched to his short, stocky body, a thick and muscular bulkiness gone urban soft and edging over his belt.

I forget how he started the conversation. I think he asked if I came to Changes often, some question that wasn't too intimate or original. He introduced himself with a firm handshake as Joey. No last name, nothing too specific or identifying. He worked across the lake in Bellevue as a loan officer in a bank. Telling me even that much made him squirmy. He clearly hadn't been out for long, or hadn't dealt with it well. He was still afraid of being caught with his hand in the cookie jar.

Joey didn't suggest throwing darts, or playing a game of pool, or going back to my place. The conversation struggled

Changes

and died, like a dinosaur in the tar pits. But he didn't go away. He seemed to have something on his mind, and was loitering in my vicinity to achieve it. Finally he took a step closer and moved his lips guardedly up to my ear.

"I was wondering if I could take advantage of you."

For an opener, that was an improvement. "You got my interest."

He cracked up. "I want to go out to the back patio, because I feel like getting some fresh air, but I don't know anybody out there tonight."

The request was implicit. "Sure, I'll go out there with you."

Joey and I looked at each other, and that was that. We both got up at the same time and circled around the pool table to the back door.

The patio was cooling down with the coming night, but the breeze had no sting. It was a warm, moody goodbye to summer, a last sweet taste of a balmy evening. Several shadowy clusters of guys dotted the patio, with muted laughter, murmuring voices. My eyes adjusted to the dark. We sat together on the far bench, working industriously at our drinks, pretending to be interested in looking up at the stars.

My thigh touched Joey's thigh. He didn't respond.

"Well, it's been a pleasure sitting out on the patio with you, and I don't feel used at all. Honest." I kissed my fingertips and raised them in oath. "May God strike me down with lightning if I'm lying."

Changes

I thought I was being light, but I guess I wasn't.

"I probably should make a confession," he said. "I'm one of those old-fashioned guys you'd call a believer."

Ouch. What a way to crush my hopes for a light-hearted night. That explained the guarded lack of response, though not what he was doing in a gay bar. I smiled, and tried to be a good sport. "You sound like a Catholic intellectual."

"Actually I'm a Lutheran."

"Oh. And what does God think of your behavior tonight?"

"He's not too happy about it."

We both chuckle.

"I don't come here often."

"I would think not," I said guardedly. "God might not approve."

"He's as confused as I am," says Joey. "While I'm at it, I might as well make one more confession." He took a deep breath, and blew it out. "I'm not only a Christian, but I'm straight."

That took a second for me to digest. "You're what?"

"I know, I know, then what am I doing here? That's what I ask myself. It's the only gay bar in Seattle I've been to. I'm not gay. I'm going to find the right woman and settle down. But sometimes, sometimes…"

He undressed me with his eyes.

"I mean, it's just a matter of time. I'm going to meet the woman I'll marry." He said the words fervently, with conviction. "That's what I want. A wife, a family. That's why I believe in God. My believing is the reason it's all going to happen. You can't have hope without God. Hope means believing that God will makes things better."

"I disagree," I said with a confidence that surprised me. "You don't need believing in God to have hope. I have a great deal of hope, and very little faith in anything. God isn't a necessary ingredient. Hope is empirical. Hope is a scientific reality."

He laughed, a short, startled bark. "Hope isn't scientific."

"Check it out. Hope is a statistical reality." I leaned forward, and used my hands to explain. "Some of the time things go right. Some of the time things go wrong. The very fact that things have gone right *some* of the time convinces me that, in the future, that same pattern will apply. Things will continue to go right some of the time. See? Perfectly logical grounds for hope. Along with the bad, some good things are coming. It's a statistical certainty. Things have to get better. Sooner or later they always do."

I could see he wasn't used to being challenged. I should have backed off right there. Now I'd rattled him.

"Sorry," I said. "Don't mean to be intense. Let's go back to flirting and leave philosophy out of it."

His handsome face remained humorless. "I just want to make one thing clear," he said. "I don't want to be rude, but we're not going to have sex. I'm not here for sex."

Changes

For a guy who was systematically squeezing all fun and life out of our conversation, he'd managed to wring out one more squeeze. "Okay," I said. "Sure, that's fine. Whatever you think. Funny, us guys, straight or gay, doesn't matter, we always think about sex first, set up our terms. Especially if you're gay. We're the culture of desire."

"What's that supposed to mean?"

"We're the minority that's defined by its desire. Not by the land we're from or the color of our skin or our size or our age or our religion. We're defined by what we find desirable. We're men who desire men. Our desire is our defining characteristic."

"That's not true at all," he objected. "That's not what being gay is." He was suddenly indignant, personally threatened. I found myself mildly surprised at what a huff he was in. "A gay man is just a man who has gay sex. That's what gay means. It's simple. It's something you do."

"Not at all," I had to contradict him. "Being gay, that's a state of mind, but there are also gay actions, which can be completely different. That's what you're talking about. A gay man can be closeted his whole life, and still be gay without ever touching another man. A straight man can have gay sex a couple times each year, and still be a genuinely straight guy who only admires women. Your nature is your general state, but your actions are separate. Sometimes they're both the same, but not always. Actions are where freedom comes in. Actions can be surprising."

Changes

"You've got it all wrong," he said with a tight smile. "What you call gay thoughts, I call temptations. They don't count, as long as you resist them. What counts is what you do. That's what you burn in hell for."

The way he said it, I could see that arguing was useless. He needed that belief for his foundations to remain solid. I backed off. I'd given him enough to think about, maybe too much. Thinking isn't sexy, and he hadn't come there to think. I'd probably talked myself right out of a night's fun.

"Well, nice to meet you," he said, giving me a firm handshake and confirming my fears. "I'm taking off. Have a good one."

That was that. He hustled around the patio heater and back into the tavern. I'd just seen the last of the mysterious Joey, the loan officer from Bellevue. It was my own fault. Troubled guys like that don't want their ideas shaken. I'd made him suspect that those thoughts he's always written off as temptations might be his real nature shouting.

I stayed a while longer, listened to Lance rattle on about Intelligent Design, chatted a while with Colby about Country Western music, listened to Jude pour out his woes over a jobless housemate who wouldn't move out. When my straw started sucking at ice cubes, I set my drink aside, said goodnight to my friends on the patio, and headed back inside to get my jacket off the coat rack.

Joey was standing by the dartboard, waiting for me.

Changes

When I approached him, he took me by the shoulder and whispered in my ear, "Remember what I said about no sex?"

"Right," I said, immediately defensive. "I never mentioned the subject. I kept my hands to myself. I didn't even have bad thoughts."

"Well, I've changed my mind. Do you live near here?"

"A couple miles away. Walking distance."

"I'll give you a lift home."

Ten minutes later Joey and I would be at my house, where we would pounce on each other and experience gloriously-animal pleasure beyond my wildest expectations, session after session of sensual excess throughout the night in a hurricane of beefy enthusiasm. With each new grope and thrust, that confused Lutheran straight boy would destroy all my preconceptions about the physical appetites of people with religious convictions and lay an even firmer foundation for the logical expectations I would continue to call hope.

Changes

WE DON'T PLAY TRIVIA

Suddenly this big guy sits down next to me on the bench and says to me, "You're my team."

He's actually about twenty years younger than me, but half a foot taller and a hundred pounds heavier, one huge walking mass of meat. Okay, you'd have to say he's overweight. But he carries it, the shoulders of an ox, everything in proportion, and he's got a classic head to top it off. His black hair is slicked back in Fifties greaser style, and he walks like he's got two six-guns strapped to his hips. You want to laugh him off, but he's got his damned charm.

I laugh. "I'm not anyone's team."

I was aware that Thursday at Changes was trivia night, and I'd always avoided Thursdays there for that reason. Trivia always sounded corny to me. To my amazement, the place was packed. I expected the big guy to move on but he just kept looking at me, like he didn't understand that I was declining. What could I say to get through to him? "I don't play trivia."

"Brilliant!" he cries, raising both arms into the air as though I'd just kicked a field goal. "That's the name of our team. We Don't Play Trivia."

"But..."

Changes

"I'll pay." He held out the dollar bill to the registrar, and gave him our team name. I shrugged and chuckled. What could it hurt?

That's how I met hulking, good-humored, Kodiak bear-sized Max. Two weeks ago, at the end of September, sitting on that bench on the other side of the pool table, I wasn't aware of Max at all. I still don't know where he came from. I was busy watching someone else completely, that slim, handsome Mexican in the black T-shirt playing pool by himself.

And then suddenly there's Max, sitting next to me thigh to thigh, talking in my face. He was like one of those big puppies that's so happy to see you that you just give in to the clobbering paws and tongue-in-your-ear enthusiasm. Or at least, that's what I thought was happening. I thought it was sheer good energy engulfing me.

Our team won. I was the only one who knew that King Kong came from Skull Island. We bought a pitcher with our prize money. Since I'm not that fond of beer, Max downed the whole thing. Those big mitts of his were starting to wander all over me by the time I got up to walk home.

I went back a week later, on the following Thursday, for another trivia night. Sure enough, I found Max there on the same pool bench, but this time he had an older friend, an admirer who appeared to be delighted with Max, his arm around Max's huge shoulders, patting Max's massive thigh. I thought they made a cute couple, and told them so. Max insisted I be on their team, though James wasn't quite so keen about me joining them. Still, the very first question, "What Pulitzer Prize-winning playwright died last week in Seattle?" was mine, all mine, and I earned a tad of James' respect, especially when our team won.

I hadn't crossed paths with Max since then, and sure wasn't planning to last night. Sunday isn't trivia night.

I didn't realize Max was a karaoke fan.

Jordan and I were back on speaking terms, and he was trying to get up the nerve to sing. On his second drink, working his way toward confidence, he had insisted on playing darts. Unpredictable at the best of times, Jordan was having a jolly time doing balancing acts as he threw his darts, so that I had my hands full and never noticed Max's approach. He watched Jordan and I playing darts for a while, and soon was playing with us. He left abruptly to run out to his truck, promising to be right back. When he returned, he dumbfounded me by presenting us with a humongous brownie the size of an iPod.

"What is it?" I said, feigning ignorance. "Carrot cake?"

"My parents were hippies," he said proudly. "It's a pot brownie. I baked it myself. Go on, try it." He then went on at length about his personal key ingredient, something he concocted himself called bud butter.

Jordan and I both broke off a piece and ate it like good sports. It wasn't awful. It tasted like bad carrot cake. Max took our response as praise, and beamed proudly. He made a point

Changes

of saying he was giving us the brownie for free, and then dropped a hint that we could get him a beer. Jordan had a running tab. I got him one.

The three of us went out to the patio, huddling around the table by the trash bin gate. I smelled it right away, that sweet smoke that isn't tobacco. In a moment Jude's pipe was circling one way and Buster's pipe was circling the other. Suddenly I'm high, and it's not the brownie.

But Max has more tricks in his pocket. He digs out a knotted baggie, which his sausage-size fingers fumble open. He pulls out a green marble of a bud.

"Put this in one of those pipes," he said. Then he told us all about it, explaining that it was called G-13, a special new breed of grass, much stronger than what we were smoking, cultivated entirely through hydroponics in secret basements full of high-powered lamps and water tanks.

Max ended up stuffing the little bud into one of the pipes, which went in one direction, and may have been more potent than the other pipe, which went the other way. Who will ever know? Max seemed to think the difference was clear. Me, I couldn't tell you. I was getting foggier by the minute.

"Just tell me if you like it."

"I like it," I said agreeably.

"Well, guess what. I can get some for you. Shit, I can get some for you tonight."

I regarded him with mild amusement. "Whatever gave you the idea that I wanted to buy some?"

Changes

"Oh, just a look in your eye." He winked at me. "Just instinct. Tell me I'm wrong. Tell me that if I could hook you up with some of this new super-grass, you wouldn't want any. Go on, I'm waiting."

He had a compelling argument.

The theme music for karaoke started up inside, and I'm up on my feet and ready to go inside, since Marcus always goes first and I'm a big fan of watching Marcus perform. I want a good seat. As it was, Jordan and Max settled for a table that was way too far from the singer at the mike.

Max suggested that he could use another beer. We put it on the tab.

Jordan surprised me deciding the time had come to try singing. He belted out, "Crazy Little Thing Called Love." I used that as my opportunity to move. Max came with me. He stood behind me, and did a lot of massaging and stroking and, well, fondling and groping. Halfway through my Long Island, still high from three kinds of pot, I was pretty passive and just about anything felt good.

He whispered in my ear that he'd like another beer. Out of nowhere Jordan put it on his tab.

But Jordan also closed his account. He was through for the night. I was having too good a time to leave, so Jordan and I hugged goodbye outside the tavern. Then Max and I went back out to the patio.

He nudged me with his big palooka elbow. "Get out that little bud of G-13."

Changes

"No," I hissed back. "Let's save it for later. I don't have a dealer anymore. My guy moved to Shanghai. I've been living in the straight world."

"Welcome back," said Max. "Your problems are solved, now that you've met me. My guy's got some right now. We could go tonight." His big paw massages the tense cords of my neck. "How much longer do you want to stay?" he asks quietly. His question confounds me. Yes, he's fondling me, he's giving me a stiffie but now I see that he expects to go with me.

"I'm getting ready to leave now," I tell him.

"I'll walk you home," he offers.

"You'd be welcome to," I say, "but it's two miles."

"Maybe I'll give you a lift home in my truck, instead. I'll be right back." He heads out to his truck again, and returns with another bud brownie. "Let me sell this real fast, to get us enough money to buy gas."

Now, I've got seven dollars in my pocket. Obviously I could contribute something. But when I say what I've got, he says, "Fine," and takes it all. "That saves having to find a buyer. Here, have the brownie."

"How'd you get into the brownie-making business."

"Living on the commune. I grew up on brownies. My Mom's bud butter is much better than mine."

I followed him out of Changes. His truck was parked down a block and around the corner. When he started the engine, it sounded like it was self-destructing, eating itself

Changes

alive. No healthy engine should roar so loud. As I pulled shut my door and fastened my seat belt, I found myself filled with sudden doubt. Would this be my last ride in this lifetime? What was I doing here?

With a lurch, the truck took off down the block. He was going much too fast, his engine roaring so loud neighbors were surely throwing open their windows in rage. The speed island loomed straight ahead. I flinched, arms ready to protect my face from the shattering windshield. Instead, he gave the wheel a sharp turn. He was drunk and stoned and reckless. I was scared. What was I doing in this truck with a maniac? We were heading straight for hell.

We couldn't get far without gas, however.

Grumbling and sputtering, the truck veered off the road into a gas station lot. While Max was inside, I could look through the driver's open window across the cab. A fraternity boy came staggering out of the gas station's mini-mart with three cases of beer. Max immediately engaged him in conversation, and came away clapping his hands in glee.

"I just sold some more pot!" he chortled. "This is great. I was totally out of money. Don't worry. Yours will be the big one."

He drove through the fraternities and sororities to my place, took one look at the stairs leading up to my apartment, and asked if I'd just get the money and bring it down.

"You don't happen to have an extra forty, do you?" he asked. "Because then I can just pay the dealer, get the stuff, swing by the frat, and head straight back here to pay you back and take care of you."

I did have an extra forty. Better than that, I ran up and got the eighty dollars I'd tucked away in my underwear and trotted back down the stairs, handing it to Max through the window. He gave me a big tongue-filled kiss and the truck roared away up the quiet street.

I waited for him to return.

I woke up sprawled across the bedspread like I'd been shot. It was two in the morning. I'd fallen asleep listening for the hellish thunder of the truck that never came back.

Changes

THOSE WERE THE DAYS

They're singing those damn love songs again.

No matter who gets up there tonight, no matter what song is sung, they all seem to be singing directly to me. Well, they can stop right now. I don't buy that malarkey anymore. Sure, my eyes get wet, but that doesn't mean anything. Torch songs and sad love ballads always get to me. Tonight they're just getting to me worse. As Earl and Jude, Colby and Buster each take the karaoke mike and make the tavern walls tremble with bitter lessons learned by the human heart, I'm more vulnerable to the words, more susceptible to the heartache, or maybe just a little more drunk.

Shawn does fix a strong Long Island.

I managed to keep it all choked up inside until Marcus started belting out "Those Were the Days." It dug up more buried pain than I expected. My eyes glazed over with a wet film and I stopped seeing what was in front of me.

I don't remember who sang after that.

Some hurts get buried so deeply you forget about them. I didn't realize the scars I still had until Marcus started singing that song.

Changes

The one pool table at Changes had been closed down, the floodlights were focused, the sound system all wired and the mike volume adjusted. At shortly after nine o'clock the music started, announcing that karaoke was only minutes away. October winds had been getting nippy, and the coat rack behind me was bulging with bulky jackets. Most of the regulars had hurried in early, pored through the volumes of song selections, made their choices, and sung their first selection.

Marcus always started off each round casually turning away from his elaborate switch-board with mike in hand, and the second set was no exception. "Those were the days, my friend," belted the handsome, barrel-chested little Sicilian. Marcus was the karaoke host, traveling from gay bar to gay bar throughout Seattle depending on the night of the week, with the city's best sound system and his own liquid-smooth, tavern-filling baritone. In another lifetime, he was a Broadway star. "We thought they'd never end."

But those days ended.

Admittedly, I was a little shaken up to start with that night. The music just aggravated emotions that were already a little high-strung. I was in Changes, all right, but a part of me was still psychologically stalled about an hour ago, sabotaged by an unexpected visitor at my house who had transformed my mood from one of happy anticipation to one of troubled bitterness about the fickle instability of love.

Changes

Let my romantic friends sing what they want. Sustained loving is a human impossibility. People who tell you they're in love, they're just working themselves up into a trance over nothing.

Just as I was leaving my house tonight for the walk up here, I was caught off-guard by a knock at the front door. I heard the clearing of his throat before I got close enough to see who was there. I had to let him in. After all, he had been the major love of my life, the object of twenty years of sexual obsession. Love lost is a cold and dead thing, but it deserves respect. Tonight he had stopped by my house on a pit-stop. This was the man I thought I would love forever.

"You feel like having a little dinner?" he suggested.

"I've eaten," I said coldly. He knew that. I would have eaten hours before. "I'm leaving."

"You have a dollar you can spare?"

There's an icy silence. Of course I have a dollar I can spare. That's not the point, is it? But this was what it had come to – the great passion of my thirties and forties, a guy who makes three times what I do, reduced to desperate stop-overs on the nights the local churches don't have charity meals. He's hoping I'll once again shell out three or four dollars for him to run down to McDonald's and buy little dollar burgers. I reach in my pocket. How can I live with myself otherwise?

When I met him, Tom Webber was seventeen, a lost, needy high-schooler with a heartbreakingly gorgeous body, a

Changes

box-boy at the local supermarket who started coming over to my house, smoking dope in the shelter of my porch, spying on my boyfriend and me, asking for back massages, leaving his shirt unbuttoned, pulling it off at the least excuse.

I was spellbound. I went right off the deep end over him. I lost my boyfriend, and hardly noticed. For twenty years I was his sexual slave, for seven of those years housing and feeding him. I have over four hundred photos of him lying naked on the bed. He was my obsession. I lost all self-esteem during those years. I never noticed it was gone. But puffing on grass had led Tom to cocaine on weekends, and weekends soon swallowed up the rest of the week in long, sweaty nights of indulgence. By the time his family staged an intervention, he was impervious to treatment. The night he came home from the abuse institute he left cocaine behind and descended into addiction to crack.

Now, this gaunt scarecrow looking at me out of the ruins of a once flawless body is that same treasured man. His clothes flutter baggy on him, since his body has exhausted every cell of fat. His handsome face is skeletal. He's carrying a couple bags, like a homeless person. I had assumed they were all charity food until he fumbled around inside one and pulled out a bulky blue fleece.

"Would you look at this sweater? My brother gave it to me. I've worn it once. I'll sell it to you for five dollars."

"Keep the sweater."

Changes

"I need to sell it," he snaps. He immediately realizes that anger is the wrong tactic, and becomes defensive and apologetic. "I've been making some stupid decisions. I wrote some bad checks."

He's just come back from two months in Canada at a treatment center. His wealthy brothers paid. He's been home one month. Without intending to, I explode with anger. "Shit, didn't that clinic teach you anything? I can't believe you. I'm afraid to ask how much."

"Nine hundred."

"You idiot." He makes me so mad I tremble. "Do you plan on eating in churches for the rest of your life?"

He misses the whole point of what I'm saying. "None of the churches have free meals tonight."

But now I realize the situation is probably worse than I think. "I hope your rent is paid."

"I'm a little behind. I didn't pay last month's rent. But I've given my landlord a check to cash next month."

"Will it be good?"

He picks at a scab on the back of his knuckle. "Not completely. Most of it will."

I let it go. This is not my battle. If I don't let it go, I'll lose it. "I hope work is going well."

"Things are okay. My review wasn't as good this year."

"I hope you're not doing what you used to do." He had developed a nightmarish habit shortly before his family sent him to Canada of dipping into the petty cash fund, and then

Changes

suffering wild anxieties that he'd be caught and fired if someone didn't loan him the money to replace it.

"A little."

"You idiot. A little missing money is all it takes."

"It's nine dollars short."

"Listen," I snap. I'm so angry I grab him by the front of his shirt and the strange thing is that he lets me. "There are two things you need if you want to enjoy your damned crack – you need a job to pay for it, and you need a house to do it in. Can you read me? Am I reaching you? Lose this job and you'll make about one-fifth as much doing blue collar labor. Are you going to be happy doing one-fifth the amount of crack?"

I could see that, sadly enough, I was terrifying him.

"And if you lose your apartment, you'll be doing your crack in parked cars and in alleys. Think you'll enjoy it as much in the rain?"

The look on his face was so harrowed that I stopped.

"Keep the sweater. You'll need it. It's going to be cold soon." I pulled a couple dollars out of my pocket. "Here. Go get some burgers. I've got to go."

He gave me a bear-hug, thanking me repeatedly, making all the usual promises, and then hustled off down the stairs toward McDonald's, clearing his crack-ravaged throat all the way down the street.

This was the man I once loved. This was the god whose body I worshipped for almost twenty years.

Changes

I read somewhere that 95% of all songs are love-songs. As the tavern comes back to life around me, Jude is at the mike belting out an old Fabian song, "Crazy Love." Crazy is the word for it, all right.

I wipe the back of my hand across my eyes, and try to forget about Tom and his dollar burgers. I'm here to meet new guys and regain my self-esteem. If love happens, I'll try to let it be natural, without promises, free to change. Love is such a temporary state. We spend most of our lives insanely chasing after a mental condition that constantly unravels and dissipates, a chemical brain rapture that can't last because it's always changing.

But we want it. We long for it desperately. There's nothing more human than sacrificing everything for it.

It's an insane hunt. But it's the only hunt there is.

That's why I'm here in this bar right now, undaunted by a lifetime of failures and mistakes, trying not to be cynical or negative, listening to my new friends sing love songs.

Changes

DOUBLE HEADER

An exceptionally ugly guy was serving drinks.

He had deep wrinkles carved into his cheeks, a grotesquely bushy mustache, and was scowling like a caricature of the biker from hell. I must have been gaping at him as I slipped through the propped-open door because he stuck out his tongue at me. Everyone down at the far end of the bar burst out laughing. Then the guy pulled off his face. It was Earl the bartender, clowning around at the end of his shift, and delighted that he'd fooled me.

"I'm ready for Halloween," he said. Then he pointed at my chest and said, "Long Island." He knew my drink. I had taken the first step in bar identity.

I drifted back to my usual spot against the wall, right where the room widens to accommodate the pool table. Since it's the bottleneck of the tavern, which was starting to get congested, I hauled myself up out of the way onto the metal bench above the coolers.

Sitting up on the metal shelf, idly watching a rock video on one of the suspended screens above the bar, I had been sipping my Long Island, minding my own business, keeping my feet out of the way of guys passing back and forth, taking

Changes

my drink slowly and letting the night happen at its own pace. Earl ended his shift. Shawn took over bartending.

None of the patrons at Changes were sitting at the three round tables by the door, and that was where Earl headed next, armed with his scissors and staple-gun, to continue decorating.

Though I already knew of his Halloween enthusiasm, I'd underestimated its extent. Chains of devil masks and witch hats and black cats with stiffened tails were not enough. He had been spending his nights off hanging more loopy cobwebs and black streamers to heighten the Halloween look. Giant spiderwebs were now drooping over the pool table, and the hunky bartender was hard at work on creating some new Halloween effects over the three dining tables.

His prison-hardened masculinity was a sharp contrast with his glee for decorating. I was pondering manly, confident Earl wielding scissors and crepe paper, draped in white boas of spiderweb, when a hand gripped my shoulder.

"What do you think of my graveyard?" said Earl, jolting me back to the real world. "Come over here and take a look." I regained my cool, slid down off the shelf, and allowed him to usher me over to the wall behind the tables.

He pointed up at his efforts. "What do you think?" He was in the midst of stapling up plastic gray tombstones in a goofy little cemetery. Each lightweight slab of imitation tombstone bore a carved inscription. He was standing in front of them, so I couldn't quite read them, but I expected them to be for the usual gay icons, Judy Garland and James Dean and

Changes

Marilyn Monroe. Instead, I could see that the name carved into the largest tombstone in the foreground was

TIMBERLINE

a popular Seattle gay bar that had just closed its doors several weeks before.

"It's a graveyard of dead bars," said Earl. His big hand took my shoulder and guided me up closer, where I could see some of the other names.

> The Golden Horseshoe
> Shelley's Leg
> The Brass Connection
> Spag's
> Tugs
> The Monastery

I looked for another name, and didn't see it.

"How about the Double Header?" I asked.

Earl laughed. "Can't bury that one yet," he said. "It's still kicking."

"You're kidding. It's still down there on Pioneer Square? I remember it from when I was a kid."

"Still in operation," he said with just a hint of pride. "Never closed. Oldest gay bar in the state."

The Double Header...

That's all it took, and I was gone. I didn't hear the rest of what Earl said. I could see his lips moving, but I don't know what he was telling me. The Double Header was still in operation? That name – the Double Header – those had been magic words in my childhood, long before I knew anything about sexual identity. That bar was the domain of my most frightening uncle, and the center of the very universe I was desperate to deny.

Though Uncle Carl was fiercely heterosexual, a super-macho Italian immigrant with a thick mustache and hairy forearms and a rough, scary sense of humor, he worked downtown at a bar called the Double Header, known in our vast Italian clan for its *funny* clientele. At least, that's all the adults ever said around us kids. The bar was in a neighborhood that now has been renewed and upscaled into pricey shops and trendy cafes, but back then Pioneer Square was just another name for the bottom of Skid Road. There was the Double Header, right at the foot of it. Nice people didn't talk about a place like that.

Frequently at one of the big Italian multi-family holiday dinners that punctuated my childhood, I would hear my giggly Aunt Carmen unleashing trills of laughter regarding the denizens of the Double Header. What exactly was funny remained a joke known only to adults.

Why Uncle Carl worked there I never knew.

That unsavory tavern loomed in a corner of my childhood, unknown and ominous, until one night, at the end of one of Aunt Lena's huge five-family Easter dinners, with

Changes

the younger women doing the dishes and the men slumped over with loosened belts napping in front of the television, the kids got a little too wound up and noisy underfoot. Aunt Lena was tired from a long day of cooking, needed a breath of fresh air, and decided on an impromptu solution. She shouted, "Kids, get in the truck."

Along with her five grandchildren, I jumped in the truck, too.

She drove us from Beacon Hill all the way downtown, down to the waterfront. Since my cousin Linda and I were the two eldest, we got to ride in front with my aunt, with all the other cousins in back. The reason for this was simple: Aunt Lena swore fiercely while she drove, and the little kids weren't allowed to hear her. Linda and I were thrilled, as auntie's profanity flew. She drove a little over the speed limit, straight down to the Double Header to pick up Uncle Carl at the end of his shift. Get out of her way – Auntie Lena was bringing her husband home to dinner.

My noisy cousins and I gathered in a nervous huddle on the sidewalk in front of the entrance to the notorious tavern. That was as far as kids were allowed to go. We had to wait for him to mix a last drink. I couldn't stop staring at the shadowy men inside. None of the guys looked very funny to me. The only funny one was Uncle Carl, who kept making jokes and vaulted over the bar like a stunt man in a cowboy movie and began throwing cans of Fanta Orange out through the door for each of my cousins.

Changes

And a can for me.

It came hurtling toward me.

I was so hypnotized by that glimpse of men murmuring to each other, standing a little too close together, that his shout of "Hey, Professor!" caught me off-guard. Too late I tried to catch the hurtling pop can, and only succeeded in fumbling and dropping my book as the Fanta Orange bounced and clunked past me out the door to clatter noisily on the sidewalk.

"Professor, you're not paying attention!" bellowed Uncle Carl.

That was his nickname for me, Professor, because I wore glasses that were always sliding down my nose and because I always carried a book with me. When he said the word Professor, it was not a compliment.

"You and that damned book!"

I snatched it up before he could come near it. He was always pulling my books out of my hands while I was reading, or hiding my books while I wasn't looking.

"You better learn how to catch better than that, Professor, or you'll end up down here with all the funny boys at the Double Header."

My cousins roared with laughter.

The very idea of being *funny* filled me with terror. I ran for the can of Fanta, stricken mute with shame. Inside the Double Header, the shadow men watched me. They were chuckling, confirming my worst fear.

I was funny.

Changes

That's my most vibrant memory of him, hurtling that can of Fanta Orange straight at me. Uncle Carl set an impossible standard of macho. He was utterly intimidating to an insecure boy like me who still didn't know the truth about himself. He treated his big dog, Spike, far kinder than he ever treated me.

That ferocious Rottweiler adored him. The dog was with him when he died. Uncle Carl had a heart attack while driving his truck home one night, and missed his turn. The car veered off the road, but fortunately stopped. Maybe at the very end he managed to push down on the brake. Neighbors heard Spike's mournful howls, and that's how they found the truck by the side of the road with Uncle Carl slumped behind the wheel.

Wading back through the memories of my childhood, my shoulder dragged against a piece of black crepe paper on the wall.

A push-pin tugged free.

It sprang off the wall like an angry insect and stung me on the cheek. It didn't hurt much – I only gave a little "Ouch!" – but it came within an inch of my eye, so it certainly got my attention.

And the attention of Earl. "Hey, you okay?" Grabbing me, holding me still by one hand on my shoulder, he examined my cheek. He brushed his thumb over the pinprick. It came away with a tiny red smear.

Changes

He kissed the tip of his finger, and touched it to the spot on my cheek.

"There," he said. "You'll live."

I don't remember anything after that. I don't think I ever finished that drink. I was lucky enough to walk in a straight line toward the tavern door. I felt drunk with memory, and a huge sense of loss. How I wished I could have known my uncle better! Stepping out into the chilly night, the tiny pinprick on my cheek stinging in the cold, I found myself wondering how Uncle Carl had felt about Halloween decorations.

Changes

BOOGEYMAN

When you're feeling unappreciated or rejected, when you desperately need to have a few minutes alone, the patio behind Changes once the sun goes down is a sheltered, fresh-air hideaway where you can get your scene together without everyone seeing your face. That's where I was nursing my wounds on that particular October evening, half-hidden in the shadows by the door to the trash bin. A guy could step out into the patio, coming from the brighter lights of the bar inside, and not even notice someone sitting over in the darkest corner, folded up compactly knees to chin, trying to be as small and unobtrusive as humanly possible.

One after another, guys checked out the patio and retreated back into the more populated interior.

But not Buster.

He seemed to know someone was out there, and maybe he knew it was me. Maybe Earl the bartender told him what happened, and that I was out there brooding over it and working on my second Long Island. Or maybe it was just the instinct of the hunt. Maybe his eyes were sharper in the darkness and could see an unhappy man where other guys just saw shadows.

Changes

Though he's a punk barista with a buzzcut and sideburns, Buster dresses like a straight, all-American jock in sweats and T-shirts. He's a tall, lanky redhead, with one of those elongated torsos El Greco loved to paint. A Scorpio tattoo brands the back of his neck. He's got an earring in one ear and a ring through one eyebrow. But what you notice are the eyes, as pure as a boy's, ice blue, but like ice picks, able to see through anything. He's got that pale skin of the redhead race, salted with freckles. A goofy, girlish laugh with a sudden mouthful of teeth, and then back to the sultry, sexy athlete breaking training.

Usually I see him at the bar with the guy who owns the place, so I've always assumed he was the owner's boyfriend. He's never shown a flicker of interest in me, so I'm surprised when he doesn't turn around and leave the patio like the others.

Instead he walks straight toward me.

"Mind if I smoke?" he asks with a smile. "While it's still legal."

I'm floored. Life doesn't get this good so easily. "Please do. Doesn't bother me at all," I say helplessly, like I would say to any attractive undertow that invited me to go swimming.

Sitting down next to me on the bench, he shakes out a cigarette from the pack, offers it to me, and when I shake my head, takes it himself, quickly, deftly, and lights it with a snap of a lighter that appears in his hand.

Changes

"Earl told me what happened," he says, answering the question I haven't spoken. "So who was this guy?"

I told him. He was the new kid at the bar, even newer than I am, and he seemed so lost and vulnerable, sitting at the end of the bar nervously working his way through the free peanuts, that all my sense of the karmic wheel urged me to say a friendly word. "He talked so softly I couldn't hear him," I said in my own defense. "I thought I was being a good listener. Then he pushes me away and says loudly, 'Dude, don't crowd me.' Drew a few eyes, let me tell you. Made me feel like an old ass making a fool of himself."

"You need another drink," says Buster, reaching in his pocket for money and standing up. I haul him back down again. I've had more than enough.

"Thanks, buddy," I say, "No more for me. I'm stupid enough as it is. I feel like such a dope."

"Nah, get over it," says Buster, elbowing me. "I know who he is. I've seen him hitting up different guys in here for beers."

"Please," I cut him off. "Let's not even talk about it. I'm trying to forget."

"You don't look like you're forgetting very well," he says. "That's why I came back here. To lighten things up a bit. Thought you might be getting a little heavy."

We chuckle. "Thanks."

I just had one swallow left, and I must have leaned back a little as I finished it off because something brushes my ear.

Changes

A huge spider lands on my shoulder. I wish I could say I'm totally cool with this. Instead, I give a shout, jump to my feet and knock over my drink. What was left of my Long Island goes draining away toward the garbage cans.

First I see him laughing. Then I look behind me with a shudder and see the little rubber spider bouncing on its thread.

"Halloween decoration," explains Buster. "You know Earl. He's so gung-ho." He settles back against the wall, batting away the rubber spider. "Halloween is the season, all right. It's a big holiday for me, too. Halloween has fucked me up totally. Halloween changed my life."

An awkward silence grips us. I don't feel comfortable asking, but I think he wants me to ask. "How?"

"Let's see, how can I say this?" he muses, then snaps his fingers. "Okay, answer this. When you were a little kid, were you a good little boy or a bad little boy?"

"Definitely good," I confess.

"Figured as much," he says. "I'd know your breed anywhere." He's grinning. "I didn't know the meaning of good. I was a hellion. I did *not* know how to stay out of trouble. Okay, so it's Halloween and I'm fourteen, and I'm not afraid of anything. This Halloween I'm through with trick or treating. That's for kids. This time I'm going to raise hell in my own neighborhood. So I turn over a trash can. I knock over a mailbox. I put a row of dog turds on the top stair of the apartment house. Little shit like that. You must have done stuff like that yourself."

Changes

He looked at me pointedly.

"Um, no," is all I can say honestly, looking back on my childhood Halloweens. They were safe and sane and polite.

He sighs in disappointment, and shakes his head.

"Well, most guys do. And I'd done enough of those goofy little bad-boy pranks. I wanted to do something bigger. So I was out looking for a piece of trouble. Boy, did I find it!"

He took a long, slow drag on his cigarette, summoning up the memories.

"So, first you have to know this: at the end of our street was the only house in the neighborhood that didn't mow its lawn. We called it the Fisher house, because that's what the mailman called it. He didn't think anyone lived there. Someone just picked up the mail. Shows how little he knew. We pretty much avoided the place. It was scary, I gotta admit, droopy trees and weeds and cobwebs. I hung out with a couple kids who lived around me, Eddie and Rick and Joey B. mostly, but none of us had lived around there more than a few years, so none of us knew any history about the place or had ever seen anyone go in or out. But we weren't fooled. We knew someone was in there, all right.

"Because sometimes someone turned on the lights.

"Joey B. always stayed out later than the rest of us, so he's the one who actually saw the lights. Sometimes in one room. Sometimes in another. We knew someone moved around inside, always at night. We stayed off the property, at least most of the time. It was big and creepy, a garage, a tool shed, lots of places to hide. And all that wild grass that no one mowed anymore. I mean, the house looked like shit. You'd think it was abandoned.

"Except for the lights.

"So this Halloween I'm telling you about, I'm walking past the house and there's one light in one window, that's all. Then I see some guys over on the side of the garage all hunkered together like they're up to something. I knew who they were, older kids than the ones I hung out with, Mack Espy and Dillon and Eddie's big brother, Willie, and they see me, and they motion me to keep quiet and come over and join them. I don't like the idea of messing around on the Fisher place, but I'm not going to miss a chance like this.

"I mean, it's cool as hell, because they're older, and they've got a reputation for being wild asses, and they're acting like I'm as good as they are, so of course I head over to join them. And they're all buddy-buddy with me, and I'm thinking, to hell with my old pals, I'm hanging out with these older guys from now on. And then, man, I don't know how they did it, they got us all drawing straws to see who was going to go up and knock on the door of that house, and of course I got the short straw.

"So I had to go.

"Well, it was a long way across the grass by myself. They stayed way back there on the street. But I could hear them laughing. They weren't trying very hard to be quiet. I didn't care. I was going to show them. So I got to the stairs and I didn't even hesitate, except that as soon as I stepped on the first stair, it creaked big-time, and so did the next one, and the next one, like no one ever used them anymore. Got to the door and okay, I was standing there for a second or two, just catching my breath, figuring out what I was going to do, but I was going to knock on it, I was all ready to, except that all of a sudden it just swung open.

"There's two arms reaching out for me, but there's only one hand. One hand is missing. I'm getting ready to scream.

"There's this guy standing in the doorway who looks like hell, red eyes, unshaved, in dirty underwear, only one hand. He looks like a fucking extra from a zombie movie. He says, 'Can I help you?'

"Then he comes toward me, with a little bit of a limp. I'm freaking out. I'm backing away. The one hand he's got shoots out and before I can bolt the sucker grabs me by the shirt and hauls me inside, just like that.

"Wham! The door's shut.

"It's the scariest moment of my whole fucking life. I'm so scared no scream is coming out. And you know what he does? He stares at me like he's going to eat me alive, and then the fucker kisses me. That's what he did. I was a total virgin, I'd never had sex with anyone back then. My first kiss comes from a fucking boogeyman. It blew my little mind. Then he pushed me back out on the porch and slammed the door behind me.

Changes

"Man, by the time I got back to those guys, I was so freaked out and crying they thought I'd seen a ghost. They didn't dare try to send me home after that. I got to hang out with them all night, and even drank two beers with them, so that my Dad totally spanked my ass when I came home drunk, but that was nothing. Nothing, man, because I couldn't forget that kiss."

He crushed out what was left of his cigarette, and shook out another.

"And you know what? I went back. It took me three days to get up the nerve, but I went back and this time I didn't have to be pulled in, I walked in on my own. Fortunately, he looked a hell of a lot better. He actually wasn't so ugly, he was in his forties, maybe, sorta cool face, actually. I let him kiss me again. And I let him feel me. I let him put his one hand under my shirt. Then I let him put it in my pants.

"I started going there every night. He lost his hand in Vietnam. He wouldn't talk about it. He never went outside, and you know why? The pain. He smoked pot for the headaches. He smoked it all the time, and he was totally paranoid in public. So he hid in his house and got stoned morning, noon and night, and never let anyone in. He had his groceries delivered to the garage.

"I went there for years. I would go every night I could find an excuse. He'd get me high and undress me and he taught me everything. My body never felt like that before.

Changes

You know what it's like, when it's all new. You think it can't get any better than that. You think it's love."

Buster takes a drink. Neither one of us says a word. I can hardly believe that he's trusting me so much.

"I kept going over there for almost two years, my senior year of high school, my first year at community college.

"Then I met Dewey. Kid my own age, in a couple of my classes. We went out for coffee one day, to sorta meet each other, you know, and it was three days before we pulled apart. I almost flunked out. I never went up to the Fisher house again.

"I was just a stupid kid then – I never even stopped to think how much I must have hurt him. A couple months later I was in the grocery store one night and heard the old bitch in front of me talking to the checker, complaining about the neighborhood. That's how I found out. The guy who owned the house had locked himself in the garage and left his car engine running."

He finished his drink and set down his glass. We both sat there together a while, looking anywhere but at each other. "I don't blame myself," he said finally. "I mean, not completely. He was a really sad man. Vietnam really screwed up a lot of guys. He didn't want to live much anymore. I mean, except for me. Funny the people you think are the boogeymen when you're a kid, huh? You grow up and fall in love with them."

Changes

I realized we were no longer alone. A handsome young musclebuilder in a black tanktop was standing beside us, holding a steaming styrofoam take-out in a plastic bag.

"You ready?" he said.

Buster jumped down, introduced me to Dewey, and the two of them bumped shoulders on their way out the door, to share a take-out dinner together somewhere in the happy land of couples.

I would have looked up at the stars, but the winter tarps had been dragged across the beams above us and cut off the sky and besides, I couldn't see much anyway.

Changes

LUPE'S SISTER

"*Now* where did my drink go?" I remember saying, still holding my pool cue, looking around me perplexed as once again my glass wasn't where I expected it to be. "Someone's moved my drink again."

"No one's touched your drink," said the cute little lesbian. She had just neatly pocketed the eight ball and won the game. "It's right behind you."

"No, it's not," I said indignantly. "I just checked." I turned around and looked behind me on the bench. "Hey, it wasn't there a minute ago!" I snatched it up. "This place is haunted." It was as simple as that, nothing more than a thoughtless grumble, the kind of thing you don't think twice about saying. I would have forgotten about it, except for what happened next.

Instead of taking my statement for a throwaway comment that didn't mean a thing, my pool opponent – who had just thoroughly trounced me – paused mid-step and gave me a funny look.

"It *might* be haunted," she said, looking around the bar as though assessing the psychometric, paranormal pressure. "It's old enough, so it probably *is* haunted."

Changes

"Guess we'll never know." I tried to playfully swat away the topic so we could move on to another subject.

It didn't work. I could tell, just looking at her. "You don't believe in ghosts, do you?" she said.

She slotted her cue in the rack and came over to stand beside me at the bench on the other side of the pool table. Lupe was a tough, compact little package in jeans and a button-down plaid shirt rolled up at the sleeves, a nice set of shoulders and a little bit of a strut, cute as a lean, cocky boy.

I'd been sitting on the other bench across the way, on the metal shelf above the coolers, and ended up being captivated by the two little dykes playing pool. I had watched the game as a bystander and found myself connecting with one of them, laughing with her at the near misses, cheering the long sinkers. Funny how you can almost become friends with someone just watching them play pool. She was enough like a tomboy that I found her attractive, and we both knew it. When she beat the gal she was playing and looked around for her next adversary and no one was signed up, she signaled to me.

I laughed and shook my head.

She didn't ask me again. She ordered me.

Well, a game of pool with a lesbian wasn't exactly on my agenda for the night, but something about her made me jump down off the metal bench and pick up a pool cue. She fascinated me. She could impersonate a boy almost as well as I could. Now that the game was over, neither of us wanted to say goodnight.

Changes

We were both stranded by the pool bench. The bar was thinning out. We were the only two people left at the dark end of the tavern.

"Ghosts?" I shook my head. "Believe in them? You mean like at Halloween?"

"No," she said, with a patient smile, hooking her thumbs in her belt. "The real kind of ghost. You're making fun, but I'm not. I know that ghosts are real."

It's always a tricky moment, when someone confesses to a belief that you personally don't find persuasive. It's hard to be honest and respectful at the same time. "And how can you be so sure?"

Those black eyes of hers looked right into mine. "I know because something happened to me."

"You saw a ghost?"

"No," she said, shaking her head sadly. "I never actually saw her."

Her response was odd enough that I was baffled. "If you didn't see her, how do you know?"

She gave me a toothy, guileless smile. "I'll tell you how I know. Got time for another beer? It's on me."

She had me in her power. "Sure."

I waited for her to walk over to the bar and get us a pitcher. She talked briefly with a couple of older women in leather jackets, then poured us each a glass, set the pitcher down on the pool bench, and settled in beside me.

Changes

"I come from a family of five sisters. That's a story in itself. My father kept hoping the next one would be a boy, and it never was. When my mother died, my eldest sister took over raising the girls. Rosa became our little mother, our *mamacita*. She was a bit of a bully. We four must have been something to handle. But one of my angriest memories is the way she would discipline us."

Although she didn't actually move, her body had become tense.

"Rosa was always after us for something we didn't clean. Or catching us in the middle of something we shouldn't do. When she lost her patience with us, she'd start swinging. With the others she'd spank and whack and paddle. But for me it was always one thing."

She made the motion suddenly with her free hand. It was like an ax blow.

"The chop at the back of the neck. Me, she always hit from behind, a chop between the shoulders, all of a sudden, to scare me. And you know what? It always worked. Every time it made me cry. No matter how tough I tried to be, she'd catch me off-guard and wham! I'd burst into tears of pure terror."

"She sounds like a real slave driver," I said.

"Don't get me wrong," she clarified, "I'm not saying I didn't deserve it. I was a hardheaded little troublemaker, even then." She gave me a tough half-smile that must have melted many a girl's heart. "I probably drove her crazy. Sometimes that's how you get love from your sisters. You bug them until they hit you."

I laughed.

"You never had sisters, did you? I can tell. Having sisters changes you forever, even though you grow up and go your separate ways.

"Rosa married first, and went to live in Santa Fe. One of my other sisters bought the house. We all go back every year for the holidays, drag our husbands along. That's the only time I really saw Rosa, every Christmas.

"Last year I went to a business conference in Santa Fe, and I decided to visit her. She lived alone. Her husband was dead. I'd never been to her apartment. Once I got to the conference, though, I found out Rosa lived farther away than I thought. I would have to take a bus from the hotel. My schedule was tight. Besides, she didn't realize I was in Santa Fe. She would never know.

"So I didn't go visit her.

A tremble in Lupe's voice was making it hard for her to go on. She folded her arms stubbornly across her chest, stared away from me and sniffed, refusing to let herself get emotional, steadying her voice by sheer force of will.

"A week after the conference I got a phone call that Rosa was dying. Of course, I took the first flight out. I got there just as they were pulling the plug. I never got a chance to say goodbye.

Changes

"I didn't cry at the funeral. I couldn't. I was so wracked with guilt that everything knotted up inside me. Everyone else was sobbing. Me, I was a rock.

"After the graveside service, when we got back to the house, my second sister took me aside in the kitchen. She's a *curandera*, know what that is?" She didn't wait for me to nod. "Someone who studies the old ways of healing.

"'There is a knot of pain inside you, Lupe,' she said. She could see what was troubling me, just by looking at me. 'You didn't know it was your last chance to see her. You love her. She knows it. Stop holding all your pain inside. Let it out. Forgive yourself.'

"But I couldn't forgive myself. And I couldn't cry. I was miserable all day after the funeral. That night I slept upstairs in my old childhood bedroom. I was catching a flight home in the morning.

"It was late. Everyone was in bed. The house was silent. I heard something in the hallway outside, on the landing between the bedrooms.

I went out, thinking maybe it was one of my sisters, maybe she couldn't sleep. She might need to talk, or just cry on my shoulder.

"'Who is it?'

"Nobody answered.

"'Who's out there?'

"No one was there.

Changes

"I stood in the dark hall, trying not to make a sound, holding my breath. I couldn't see anyone. Then I heard someone come up behind me.

"Wham! Something hit me hard, a physical blow.

"A chop to the back of my neck.

"I spun around. No one was there. I was alone in the hall. I burst into tears, just like a little girl. It was her. She always knew how to make me cry."

Changes

QUEEN OF THE FAIRIES

Pretty women make me nervous. I'll admit, I was standoffish at first. I always am. I presupposed that she had expectations I was not going to meet. I did what I always do. I pretended like I didn't notice her.

But I noticed her plenty from the very first moment I saw her. I'd been sitting out in the patio under the hanging plants, wedged between the bare, black arm of Jude and Buster's bony shoulder, leaning against the back wall looking up at the stars, on that last summer night before the tarp was drawn over the patio beams for the winter. She walked out of the lighted bar and crossed the twilight patio in a cloud of smoke straight toward our table. It seemed like Michelle Pfeiffer or Nicole Kidman had stepped down off the movie screen to have a personal word with us.

I immediately looked away. I don't stare at women like that. I figure they're stared at enough. She had straight, blond hair, porcelain skin, soft blue eyes, perfect elfin features. She was followed by her bald, musclebound boyfriend, who was forcing a smile and trying to put a good face on being there. He sported all the usual features wrapped up in a showy, skintight T-shirt, but to my surprise it wasn't the hunky boyfriend everyone was hugging. It was her.

I leaned over and whispered in Jude's ear, "Who is she?" Before he could answer, she'd walked up to him and he swept her into his arms. After a long embrace and many murmured endearments, she went on to the next old friend.

"That's Yvonne," said Jude.

"She's not a lesbian, is she?" Somehow it was clear she wasn't, but I asked anyway.

"Nope, she loves men just as much as we do," he said. "But she likes to be in charge. So she comes here. Plenty of men, and nobody hitting on her. When you look like she does, horny men can be a hassle. Here she's got all the men and none of the problems."

She was a favorite there, all right. Not because she was particularly witty. Not because she bought everyone drinks. She just seemed to be unnervingly lovely and to know everyone's name and to have a kind word for every person she greeted.

Why did they all like her so much? It seemed immoderate and irrational, as though she were casting a spell from which I was exempt. I would never have guessed that the night was coming when I would side with Yvonne against most of the other people in that bar.

It happened on Halloween. That year was a trick-or-treater's nightmare, a drizzly, dripping night to ruin costumes and make cosmetics streak and run. The indoor malls were

Changes

jammed with little devils and ballerinas, while the streets gleamed wet and empty.

Changes had been in the mood for weeks, anticipating that night. The little bar was packed. Giant spider webs loomed over the pool table. Every wall and corner had its plastic ghoul or skeleton, paper pumpkin or cardboard cat. Already a huge Pooh bear sat on a stool at the bar downing a rum and Coke. Two very pregnant nuns in full habit sat beside him, keeping their wooden rulers busy slapping the palms of all the bad boys. A scholar in graduation robes was sharing a pitcher with an intern in his green scrubs and a hooker in a shiny red dress. A stubbly-faced wolf with a hairy belly was poorly disguised in sheep's clothing.

Earl the bartender had personally transformed the tavern with his elaborate Halloween decorations, but there was no sign of him. Behind the bar, assisted by a cowboy in full rodeo gear and a young sailor boy, between the spigots and the cash register where Earl should have been mixing drinks, stood a tall, husky woman with a tossled mane of green hair falling about her shoulders. Then she coughed, a hacking, wretched sound, and I saw the chest hair between her breasts.

"The usual?" said the voice of Earl out of moist, red lips.

I smiled affirmatively. "That cough doesn't sound good."

"I'm not doing too well tonight," he confessed, tossing his green hair back over his shoulder with a practiced turn of the head while shoveling ice cubes into a glass. "I came down with something. I should be home in bed." He coughed again to make his point. "But I didn't want to miss Halloween. It's my favorite holiday. And Twyla only comes out once a year. So she's here, all right, high heels and all. She may feel like shit, but the show must go on."

Something happened behind me, out of our sight range. When people started turning toward the door, I didn't understand why. Then Twyla leaned sideways to look, as well, and so I turned, too.

The Queen of the Fairies was entering Changes.

It was Yvonne, in a costume that demanded to be noticed. Her gossamer gown was varying shades of blue, and barely came up high enough to cover her breasts. Her hair was also blue, but with a metallic shimmer, and she wore turquoise slippers and was crowned with a blue tiara, so maybe she was really the mysterious blue fairy who watches over Pinocchio, but her outstretched wings were magenta pink and so big that she had to turn sideways to get through the bottleneck between the bar and the coolers.

She was followed by her showpiece boyfriend costumed as Pan, with little horns on his bald head, leggings of mock goat hair, and a string attached to his big teddy bear of an erection that should have boinged straight up with a jerk of the string. The string wasn't working. No matter how much he tugged, his floppy woolen dong refused to rise.

Changes

I was just carrying my drink away from the bar, looking for a good place to plant myself so that I could see the contest, when I noticed three soccer players at the end table waving at me. All three were buff young Latinos wearing identical trunks and black-striped athletic jerseys, but one had red stripes on his jersey, one had green stripes, and one had yellow. With them sat an elegant Asian woman in a sheer black dress, chopsticks jabbed through her hair, playing idly with a nail file that looked like a dagger.

The soccer star in yellow looked terrifyingly familiar. Then he stood up and waved his muscle-bound arms, and I recognized my former best friend. I was so unprepared to see Jordan at Changes that at first my mind refused to register who he was. This was my domain. I had grown into someone different here. I had learned to be without him here.

With him were the two new pals who now took up all of Jordan's time, his Chilean playmates, Eduardo and Ismael. Eduardo, the red soccer player, all shoulders and cockiness, had been Jordan's summer passion, the reason I'd been forced to fend for myself and start walking to Changes. The green soccer player was Ismael, Eduardo's lover, the reason Eduardo had travelled to the United States. Ismael was high maintenance, suspicious, and Machiavellian, but lovely as the dawn. He had come along to make sure there was no hanky-panky. Together the three of them shared underwear and cell phones, and were capable of entangling their hot young passions in an infinite number of secrets, betrayals, and melodramatic confrontations. It was a hot, spicy brew bubbling dangerously near the top.

"Sit down, sit down, we've been waiting for you," slurred Jordan. "Finally a happy face. These two idiots have been fighting all night." The two Chileans scowled. They both seemed to be pouting, like sullen magazine models who are unhappy about being gorgeous.

"Shut up, Jordan," said Izzy. Underneath the playful surface of his classic Renaissance face was a seething dragon of rage. He pretended to smile.

"Don't tell him what to do," snapped Eduardo.

"Nobody asked for your opinion," barked Izzy.

"Give me patience," sighed Lucy, stretching her elegant neck as she smoked. "These two are driving Jordan and me to drink." She sounded much less drunk than Jordan, who I could see was actually quite plowed. Lucy clicked her long, black fingernails on the table. She was looking her best in sheer black, legs crossed. She was bored, which means she was dangerous. She made a signal to the bar, which Twyla seemed to understand.

"Honest, I didn't know until an hour ago that we were coming here," slurred Jordan. "I didn't feel like going out tonight, but they made me."

"Oh, really?"

"Last minute decision," he said. "Impulse."

"Pretty good costumes for impulse."

"Lucy made the costumes."

Changes

"Civic Light Opera was having a sale," chimed in Lucy. "They're from an old production of *Damn Yankees*."

"But that's baseball, not soccer."

"Oh, I doctored them up a bit," she said, with a dismissive wave. "We made an extra suit. Just in case Jordan decided to come with us."

Lucy might have gone on, but the words stopped coming out of her mouth. She was looking up at the Queen of the Fairies, who was standing before our table, a vision in blue with her wings shuddering pinkly behind her.

"Great costumes, boys." said Yvonne. "I'd like to play on *your* team." Her female instinct led her to direct her next comment to Lucy. "Are you the clever one with thread and scissors?"

Lucy was flattered. "Anyone could have done it," she said dismissively, confident that no one in Seattle could match her. "Your costume is the one to beat. Where did you rent it?"

"I didn't," said Yvonne. "I sewed it myself."

Twyla delivered a drink to our table, and coughed her way back to the bar. Lucy slid the drink across the table toward Jordan, who put up only a feeble resistance before grabbing the glass and finishing it off all at once.

Smiling at me with complicity, as though we'd concocted some kind of mischief together, Lucy leaned closer to Jordan but said loudly enough for us all to hear, "Won't be long before Jordan shows us his special Chilean soccer boy dance."

Changes

Twyla stopped in her tracks behind the bar. "Excuse me," she said into the microphone that suddenly appeared in her hand, amplifying her voice to fill the tavern, "but it sounds like we have a little entertainment in store this evening. What dance is this?"

Jordan thrust out an arm to prevent Lucy from continuing, but she batted it effortlessly aside. Nothing could stop her now. "It's the dance the boys in Chile do in the showers when the soccer game is over," cried Lucy, a little too loudly.

"Oh, my goodness!" said Twyla, fanning herself in excitement with fluttering, blood red-polished fingertips. "And we get to see this dance? When? when? when?"

Heads are turning now. Suddenly Jordan has the attention of everyone around him. He's drunk enough to want to keep it, so he stands up and obligingly pulls off his jersey.

That's all it takes. Nothing is quite as effective as a little bare skin to grab the attention of a gay audience. His shirt removal causes a gasp all around him. Suddenly heads are craning to see. There's applause, hoots, whistles, clapping and stamping and encouraging cheering.

"Striptease!" cries Lucy with mischievous glee. The cry is quickly taken up.

Both Eduardo and Ismael have experienced an abrupt sea change in mood, obviously think the idea of Jordan making a fool of himself is great good fun Chilean-style, and find themselves suddenly harmoniously talking Spanish to each other and pushing Jordan away from the table toward the bar, where Twyla is clearing a place at one end.

That's how it happened.

Suddenly Jordan is climbing up onto the counter, right there in the middle of all the Halloween festivities, the music is turned up, the house beat is thudding in the walls and floor, and to my horror Jordan is loving every minute of it, getting more and more provocative, threatening to pull down his trunks, showing us the crack in his butt, then lower, then lower, with a wiggle and a twitch and a thrust.

Well, they love it.

Strangely enough, I find myself feeling sad. This is my neighborhood bar, where I'm comfortable. Pretty boys showing off their bodies belong downtown in the discos. Jordan is pulling down his trunks, showing his jockstrap, and they're all going berserk. You can see he's just riding on the high. He swings his arms up above his head in sheer dancing exuberance, and knocks one of the ceiling panels loose. Suddenly a white slab of plywood teeters out of the ceiling, slides loose and starts to fall. Jordan catches it, shoves it back up into place, and keeps right on dancing to finish the song.

Which gets a huge applause.

Amid a last flurry of drink orders, riding on the excitement sweeping through the crowded little tavern, Twyla announces grandly, "Let the costume parade begin!" One by one, encouraged by clapping and appreciative cries, every customer wearing a costume begins to slowly promenade around the pool table.

We cheer them on.

As the Queen of the Fairies majestically strolls around the pool table, she raises her fairy wand and blows out a stream of bubbles upon all her subjects. Surrounded by bubbles, a vision of loveliness, she brings down the house.

It can't get any louder, it seems, but then here comes Jordan, just wearing his trunks and yellow athletic socks. Instead of parading around after the others, to everyone's surprise he jumps nimbly up on top of the pool table and begins rolling around bare-bodied on the green felt, striking one provocative pose after another, and then springs off, athletic, bare and beautiful, the consummate performer.

They roar.

It's not long before Twyla announces that it's down to two finalists – the soccer player and the queen of the fairies. This is where the night goes sour. This is a costume contest, not a striptease. Yes, she's a straight woman, but she has the best costume. No one else is even close. Why is she competing against a cute gay man showing a lot of skin?

"This doesn't make sense," I object to Shawn, the young cowpoke helping Twyla behind the bar. "I mean, it's like entering a roast beef in a pie contest. Sure, it's mouthwatering. But it isn't a pie."

"I thought you knew each other," said Shawn. "Didn't you guys used to be friends?"

Changes

His words stung.

Before I can try to explain that one, Twyla holds up her arms, and calls for the vote.

Suddenly I've got a very sick feeling. Are gay men really hardwired to only think with our cocks? I wasn't going to wait around for the results. I didn't want to know. I grabbed my jacket, said a few excuse-mes, and let the tavern door thud behind me. The wet night felt like a relief. The last thing I expected was for the bar door to creak open behind me, and for nearly naked Jordan to barge out and grab me. I got cold just looking at how bare he was.

"Hey, what are you doing?" I yelled at him. "Are you out of your mind? Get back inside, you idiot. This is a public street. And it's fucking freezing."

"Don't be mad. Please."

"Why do gay people have to be so stupid?" I pointed at him. "That's a body, not a costume."

He grabbed me and shook me. "Listen, I'm drunk. I got a little carried away. Really, I wasn't even going to enter. It was Lucky's idea."

"Go back inside. They're voting on you."

He wasn't going.

Some kinds of friendship don't die. He was everything that angered me about the gay world, testosterone-driven and superficial and faddish, self-indulgent and self-absorbed and self-destructive. Jordan Perez was utterly committed to his own pleasure. Still, I was far from perfect, with my share of shortcomings and faults. We'd been pals for eleven years. We'd learned how to put up with each other.

"I miss you," said Jordan, clinging to me, trembling.

"Right," I said. "You don't even know me. The guy you *miss* doesn't exist anymore."

"I know you better than you think," said Jordan. "You're not rid of me yet. We'll get a beer this weekend."

"Right."

"I'll give you a call."

"Right."

"You'll see."

The bar door opened. With her wings filling the doorway, the Queen of the Fairies stepped out into the rain just long enough to say, "They're waiting for you to vote."

"Thanks," said Jordan.

Before she could duck back inside, I called out, "Your costume is the best!"

She smiled, and blew a stream of bubbles toward me. Then she stepped aside, carefully adjusting her wings to make room for Jordan. Damp and shivering, he went back into the bar to wall-rattling, thunderous applause.

Changes

THREE HUNDRED ASPIRIN

I felt the guy's hand taking hold of mine before I realized what was happening.

He was sitting against the pull-tab machines, slowly working his way through a pitcher of beer, watching me make the best of my own miserable decision to go out for a game of darts with Jordan and Eduardo. What possessed me, I'll never know. How could I really have believed those two lust victims could concentrate on anything as remote as a dartboard?

The guy watching us didn't say anything, just occasionally caught my eye when I came back from my turn. Now, without warning, both of his hands took my hand between them. I was so dumbstruck I just froze, unable to think of one clever thing to say. But instead of showing affection, his hands simply pried apart my fingers and removed the three darts.

It was a slow Monday night at Changes so no one was sitting in the seats at the end of the bar, endangered by our misguided missiles. I was ahead, but that was simply because my competitors weren't concentrating on the game.

I should never have come, I knew that now. Jordan had phoned out of the blue and talked me into it, trying to fool both of us into thinking our friendship was still alive. Only

Changes

when his car pulled up at my house did I realize Eduardo was coming with us. I'd never played darts before and somehow Jordan had talked me into playing with them, since tonight there wouldn't be many witnesses to my shame. Now it turned out I had a natural flair for the sport. Besides, throwing darts at a target was better than being ignored by my two amorous companions.

Then, without a word of warning, this guy grabbed my hand and my darts.

He was bigger than me, a balding, buzzcut blond with a reddish-blond goatee and foggy, gray-blue eyes. He was just wearing a baggy T-shirt and faded, worn out jeans, sitting on the metal shelf above the coolers, slumped back beside his pitcher. The next thing I knew, he had raised one hip off his stool enough to remove his key chain from his blue jeans' pocket. Attached to his keys was a little gizmo which he snapped loose and used to straighten the rubber prong nose of each of my darts. Then he screwed tight the dart nose into each of my winged yellow plastic missiles, and gave them back to me improved and ready to throw.

I stammered out my flabbergasted gratitude.

He batted it away. He gave me a low-key smile, turned me around, and pointed me back toward the target. "It's your turn," he said. "Your friends are waiting for you."

That hardly described their activity. My friend and his new love were simply pausing. They had been indulging in bouts of wild animal sex with only occasional breathers ever since they crossed paths, and were already doing warm-up exercises for their next round. The two of them were intently living up to every stereotype of ripe, lovely, giddy, horny, touchy-feely melodramatic lovers, blind to everything else in the world except themselves. They couldn't keep their hands off each other. I threw my darts, but neither of them noticed. I could have been aiming at them.

"Are they always like this?" asked the dart fixer, draining the last of his beer and pouring himself another glass.

"One of them used to be my best friend," I said. "Love makes people stupid." My straw made a sucking noise at the bottom of my Long Island.

"I wouldn't know much about that," he mumbled. "I haven't had a date since New Year."

That was a surprise. Since that was over eight months ago, it meant he had a dating record similar to my own. Though the guy wasn't classically handsome, he was attractive in a simple, masculine way. When somebody says a thing like that to you, it sounds like an invitation. When I came back from throwing my darts, I stood a little closer.

Jordan and Eduardo pulled apart briefly to take their turns. They were lost in that unrealistic world where body heat is enough. As soon as they finished throwing, they glomped back together again like separated magnets, and I went up to throw more darts at the target. For a moment I just stood there indecisively, studying the electronic scoreboard, trying to consider which number to go for. I was having a hard time concentrating. Then I felt a body come up behind me, taller than me, warm against my back, and an arm point over my shoulder. "Go for the nine," he said.

That's how I met Foster, that big galoot of a guy, over six feet tall, two hundred pounds, a lab technician up on Pill Hill who sometimes catches a bus out to Changes for a pitcher of beer after his shift. He doesn't like hanging out in the gay district. He calls gay people flaky and sluts. "I'm one hundred percent gay," he said, "don't get me wrong. I'm just not a lying sex addict. I'm too honest. Not much honesty in the gay world."

"Not much honesty anywhere, for that matter," I amended. "Gay people don't have the market cornered on lying to have sex. But I know what you mean. I've always been sort of an outsider, too." Of course, my reasons were the exact opposite of Foster's. I don't feel superior to gays, I feel inferior. I've never felt handsome or trendy or sexually cunning enough to be officially gay. Not to mention young enough.

Maybe something about being an outsider bonded us.

He coached me through the game, and I won it. He became my coach. I stood next to his stool. I won the second game as well, to Jordan's intense displeasure, finally snapping him out of his lusty indolence. We were halfway through a very competitive third game, in which I had the complete attention of both lovestruck beauties, when I turned around to ask Foster a question.

Changes

He wasn't there.

A vanishing act was the last thing I expected. At first I thought he'd just gone to use the men's room. Then Jordan went in to take a piss, and said he wasn't there. The other bathroom was empty. I poked my head outside into the dark, empty patio. Then I checked out in front of the tavern. Maybe he's gone outside to use his cell phone. Maybe he just dashed across the street to use the cash machine or to buy cigarettes down at the Food Giant. But it was none of those. He didn't come back. He was simply gone.

I was so rattled by his sudden departure that I could hardly hit the dartboard. Jordan and Eduardo both trounced me, finished their drinks, and dropped me off at home before speeding back to Jordan's apartment to continue their sexual marathon.

Foster had somehow gotten under my skin, then vanished without a word. The gay world can be such a heartless, fickle place, with no one telling the truth. The possibilities were endless. I let it go at that.

But a few days later as I walked into Changes on a much more crowded night, Foster and I practically ran into each other. He was just leaving, heading for the door. I was so happy to see him that I convinced him to go back inside for at least a little while longer. His answer was to order another pitcher. That was what I think pushed him over the edge. Foster knows his own limits, but he'd been there since getting off work and that night he extended those limits to join me. Which was how he got himself drunk.

He slumped over one of those little tables near the front of the bar where I never sit. I straddled a stool beside him.

"You left so suddenly last time," I mentioned.

"Yeah, I almost missed my bus," he said, as though that explained it.

His hand lingered on my thigh. It seemed obvious to me that he liked me, so I started pushing a little. Which in Foster's case was the wrong thing to do. "Give me your phone number, before you vanish again."

A subtle tension crept over him, and his hand slid off of me. "Listen, I'm boring. You don't want to get to know me. There's nothing to know."

"I doubt that very much," I tried to laugh it off. "You've just finished reading *War and Peace*, you do oil paintings and watercolors in your spare time, you've got a shitload of friends who keep calling your cell phone constantly whenever I'm with you. They must like you for some reason. Couldn't we get together somewhere other than this bar?"

"You don't understand," he said. "Now is not a good time for me to be getting into relationships."

"Whoooa," I said. "A date isn't a relationship. How about a friendship?" I persisted.

"I've got enough friends," he barked at me, and then regretted it. "It's just bad timing. I've got to get my scene together first."

Changes

"You can go through your whole life postponing stuff you want to do until a better time comes along," I said, not getting the hint. "The only time you really have is now."

"Sometimes now is not the best time," he said, chugging half the beer in his glass. "Sometimes you need to heal from life first." He sighed. Either I was bugging him or persuading him. "Two months ago I tried to check out."

That snapped me out of the mating dance. I heard the click of pool balls, the clatter of glasses. He looked at me blankly, as surprised as I was.

"I can't believe I just told you that."

"Why?" I didn't really whisper the word, it was more like just mouthing it. "Why would you do that?"

"That's the funny thing. I don't know."

He looked genuinely puzzled, and maybe a little scared.

"I work in a lab, so I know what it takes to do the job. Do you realize what the most lethal over-the-counter drug today turns out to be? Aspirin. I drank down three hundred tablets."

He strained his neck, pretending to be very interested in something down beyond the end of the bar and the pool table. "Swallowing them was the easy part. I mean, how hard is downing whiskey? The hard part was waiting to die. Aspirin is slow. I had to lay there waiting all night. A lot of thoughts can go through your head in a night. The next morning a buddy of mine stopped by and found me passed out on my bed, with my pillow soaked in blood. Internal bleeding. He got me to a

Changes

hospital in time. Now he lives with me. He's in love with me. I wouldn't be alive if it weren't for him."

Maybe it was just his tone of voice, but suddenly it all came together and I got it. I looked into the sad, drunken anguish in his eyes. "And you're not in love with him?"

"See what I mean?" He gave a sad little smile that half-heartedly lifted one side of his mouth. "How do you do the right thing? It's all so complicated. That's why I say now is not a good time." He slid off his stool and stood up. "But don't get me wrong. Maybe the right time will come."

Foster walked out of the tavern without looking back.

I never saw him again.

Changes

THE PALM READER

Jude bumped past us on his way to the men's room, so I asked him. "Never seen her before."

Then Buster hurried by on his way out to the patio for a smoke, so I asked him. He threw back at me, "You sure that's a real woman?"

We were waiting at the bartender station for Earl to mix my Long Island. I leaned over the bar so the other customers couldn't hear me and asked Earl. He didn't know who she was, either. Assuming she was a she.

I couldn't let it go. Something about her was painfully familiar. I kept looking back at her table.

At first, as we came into the bar, she simply looked like any other super-size lesbian of the earth mother variety, an ample, nurturing woman waiting for someone to arrive. At second glance, however, I caught the masculine jaw, the big hands, and a hardness in the eyes that was hardly feminine. She was sprawled across her stool and half the table by the door, directly opposite the little room where Earl tends to the sizzling grill. She wore a shapeless black shift that she filled to overflowing. Her thick black hair was beyond shoulder-length, with no attempt to hide a white streak across the brow. Out of

Changes

over thirty people in those tight quarters as we walked in, why would I have noticed her alone?

Then I noticed a playing card in her hand.

"I can't believe it," I laughed, as I stood behind Jordan waiting for Earl to return his bankcard, "that woman over there is playing solitaire." We headed for the pool table to see how many guys were in line. While Jordan wrote his name on the blackboard, I glanced back.

For some reason, she kept holding up a single card. She didn't play it. She wasn't looking at the cards at all. She was peering into Earl's little grilling room. At least, that's what I thought until Earl strode out the door, carrying two platters of burgers. She didn't seem to see him. She seemed to stare right through him into outer space.

"This is going to drive me crazy. Who is she? Why does she look so familiar?" Jordan had stopped to watch the pool game in progress. Looking back over my shoulder, I walked right into him.

"Hey, watch it!"

But that's when it hit me. The way she stared into outer space finally triggered a memory and a clue. "I remember who she is now."

He took one look at my face and seemed to read my mind. "So do I!"

By now we were blatantly staring at her. She didn't appear to notice. We said it together.

"The palm reader!"

Changes

That summer our friendship had been on shaky ground, and we both knew it. In one of our attempts to revive it, I had bussed up to join Jordan at the Capitol Hill Block Party, a huge noisy annual conglomeration of booths and services and liberal people. Like an alternative street fair, it clogged one end of the Seattle gay district every summer with clowns and charities and gay boys in tanktops.

It had been a perfect hot July afternoon. Jordan and I were taking our second slow stroll through the crowded maze of stalls, picking up a pamphlet or two but mostly just enjoying all the guys with their shirts off, elbowing each other every time a good-looking one wandered into view, the usual eye candy sport of the idle gay mind.

We both noticed the sign "Clairvoyant Readings" at the same time. The sign must have been there before, on our first loop, but neither of us noticed it. Now there it was, above a card table with a white tablecloth fluttering in the breeze. Seated behind the table was that same large woman in black.

"I'm going to do it," said Jordan. He's the impulsive, reckless one, I'm the one who is careful.

"Oh God, Jordan, why? I thought we were here to have a good time and meet cute guys?"

"I want to know the right thing to do," he barked. "You keep hounding me that I'm making the wrong decision. Well, if I am, I want to know."

Changes

In a second he had slipped through the crowd of munching, chattering, staring people, tykes in hand, dogs on leashes, and landed across from the woman in black in the empty chair facing her table. I followed reluctantly, too curious to be left out.

"He's my best friend, he can listen," said Jordan, explaining my presence.

"Yes, I can see that," she said. In one fist she had a thick white cloth she was using periodically to mop her wet forehead. "I saw you go by the first time," she said to Jordan, smiling and extending her hand. "I could tell you had a big question inside. You didn't see me because you weren't paying attention. That's one of your problems, isn't it?"

I burst out laughing. It's the central problem of Jordan's life.

He gave her the money.

She took one of his hands, and held it gently in both of hers. "My name is Tamara. I'm glad you made the decision to trust me. I'm going to tell you about your future now. Before I start, I want you to think carefully. Are you sure that's what you really want?"

Something about her forthrightness gave me the chills. Until that moment it had been a game. I tightened one hand on Jordan's shoulder. If he was ready to bolt, I was right behind him. But he allowed her to continue holding his hand, palm upward. "That's what I want." Then he added curiously, "Have you always been this way? Able to see things?"

Changes

She shrugged. "I'm Romanian. It's in my blood." She dragged the cloth in her fist across the drops of perspiration lining her brow. "Now, you came to me because you're troubled about something. You want me to give you advice. What is it you need to know?"

In my memory, all the music and noise and voices of the Block Party are turned off at this point. There's an icy silence around Jordan and I as she reaches across the white tablecloth and places her other big hand on top of his, cupping his hand between both of hers as though it's the very essence of him, like a butterfly caught in a meaty trap. Then she opens up his hand like a surgeon preparing to operate, one hand holding his, one hand poking and prodding, bending back the fingers, turning the palm this way and that way so she can see every crease and line.

"I've got a wonderful boyfriend of three years that I'm falling out of love with," said Jordan. His voice actually cracked. He cleared his throat. He's smoking now, and his throat is always raw from coughing. She didn't look at him. She was looking at his palm. "And, at the same time, I've got a sexy new boyfriend that I can't get out of my mind. I'm insanely in love with him, and that's my problem. I'm at the biggest crossroads of my life. I'm about to give up everything I've worked for during the last three years with a fine, good man for this hottie I hardly know. I'm going to have to live with this decision for the rest of my life. My future happiness depends on what I do next."

Changes

She smiled at him knowingly. I saw her squeezing his smaller hand in her huge meaty ones. She gripped it and peered down into it, scrutinizing every mound and wrinkle and line. For once her lips stopped smiling and settled into a straight emotionless gash.

Slowly her eyes closed. When they snapped open, Jordan flinched backward and accidentally hit me. "You're wrong," she said.

We both looked at her mutely, waiting for her to go on, puzzled to think she could possibly consider that sufficient information.

"Your future happiness does not depend on what you do next."

Jordan's features slackened from his usual cheerful aggressiveness into a puzzled apprehension. "Why not?"

"Do you really want to know?"

"Yes"

She scowled down at his hand. "Neither one of these guys will be instrumental to your future happiness. Your decision between them is unimportant."

Jordan stared at her dumbfounded. He was about to slide his hand away from her, but she held onto it. "But I'll tell you something else," she said. "Someone else will play a role in your future happiness. Someone you already know. Someone you have known and loved for many years."

She let go of his hand.

Changes

Neither Jordan nor I looked at each other. We knew who she meant.

"But he's my best friend," said Jordan.

"*Was* your best friend," I corrected.

"*Is* my best friend," he asserted.

"Sometimes best friends last longer." She turned her attention to me. "And how about this best friend of yours? Is he ready to know what the future holds for him?"

Her black eyes could see right through me. I almost tripped backing away from her, laughing my nervous, let-me-out-of-here chuckle.

"Not me, thanks. Oh, no. I'm way too scared."

That was the last thing I said to her.

I walked to the corner, out of shouting distance, and waited in the street fair crowd for Jordan to tip her. He never mentioned the last things she said to him. I never asked. We both wandered on through the Block Party until we got hungry and went out for Chinese food.

All night long I regretted not being brave enough to hear my fortune. The next morning I phoned Jordan and told him I was ready to pay my ten dollars to hear what she had to say. We went back to the Block Party. We found the exact spot where her stall had been yesterday.

Now it was a vacant stretch of litter-sprinkled street. No one had seen her that day. We searched every alley and stall in the entire Block Party. Tamara was nowhere to be found.

Until now.

Changes

"What a coincidence," I said. That summed it up. As far as I was concerned, the situation was closed. I prudently turned my back on her and tried to nudge Jordan by the shoulders in the other direction toward the pool table. "How long is the line waiting to play?" I asked. "Don't you think it's time you chose your cue?"

"No, wait a second," said Jordan. "Come on. If that's her, I want to tell her about her prediction. How right she was."

With me following reluctantly behind him, Jordan worked his way back down the bar to the end table, where he stood directly in front of her. His being there failed to elicit the slightest response from her. This was an extremely unusual reaction to a man as good-looking as Jordan, who expects to effortlessly command attention from anyone anytime.

"Tamara," he said.

Suddenly she focused on him. She didn't move a muscle except her eyes, but all at once we had her complete awareness. This woman gave me the creeps, quite frankly, and just that little movement of her eyes would have been enough to send me running for the door. I stayed there beside Jordan out of a sense of friendship. I knew only too well how much he likes to play with fire.

"You read my palm at the Block Party," said Jordan.

"I know," she said.

Changes

Jordan is usually unflappable, but I could tell she rattled him a little. "Well, I came to tell you that you were exactly right. I broke up with my old boyfriend, and my new boyfriend dropped me. Both guys are gone now, but I still have my best friend, just like you said I would."

"Of course, you do."

She looked at him blankly, like he was speaking in a dialect she wasn't sure she understood.

"What are you trying to tell me? That I was right? Of course, I'm right. I'm always right. That's the problem, isn't it? Did you think I was just guessing?"

She sighed, and it was a kind of seismic movement that shook her body. The bar stool groaned beneath her.

"I know too much, cutie, way too much. Makes a girl want to drink."

The way she said the word "girl" raised the question again of what gender she really was. Her massive triple chin made it hard to tell if she had an Adam's apple or not, the few whiskers I spotted weren't gender conclusive, and asking was out of the question. Male or female, she was clearly not a very happy person.

"Face it, there isn't too much about love I *don't* know." She finished her drink in a gulp. "I've seen all its forms. It's not just in your palm, it's written all over you. When you've been marked by love, your wounds show. And if love doesn't want you, your prayers are wasted."

Changes

She tipped back her glass, sucking at ice cubes for a drink that wasn't there.

"I should know. I've been looking for love, and hoping for love, and waiting for love my entire life. I can see into the future, but I don't see any love there. I see loneliness, fucking loneliness, a whole lifetime of fucking loneliness and nothing else." She paused a moment, sucking in a deep breath of air to rein in a surge of anger.

"I keep waiting to see love coming for me. I keep thinking it has to be out there somewhere. I just can't see it yet. But I'm wasting my time. I see my future, and there's no love in it."

The muscular forearm of Earl the bartender appeared out of nowhere, proffering a drink Tamara had ordered by a signal too subtle for me to notice. She communicated payment by another such signal. Suddenly Jordan's name was being called, and he dashed off toward the pool table. As Earl slipped away in the other direction she locked eyes with me, so abruptly and boldly I couldn't budge.

"And how about you?" she asked, nailing me to the floor with her eyes.

"No, I don't think so," I said quickly, not sure what she was suggesting but absolutely certain I didn't want to.

"Not brave enough to take a look at your future yet? Just a little look?"

I burst into nervous laughter, my usual ploy, hoping the conversation will go on without me, which it doesn't, hoping the subject will change, which it won't. Tamara is looking at me, waiting.

"I'm afraid to know," I told her. "Sometimes the only thing that gets me up in the morning is hope. I need hope that someday my writing will be successful. I need to hope there's a guy out there for me."

"Don't you want to know?" she asked.

"No." That much I knew for certain. She was giving me the creeps again.

"Not even about your love life?"

"What if I don't get to have a love life?" I blurted out. "What if I'm like you?" I didn't say it to be mean, but I noticed she gave a tiny flinch. "Tell me, don't you wish you didn't know?"

I'm waiting for an answer. Tamara is staring down at her drink. Maybe the look on her face all the answer I'm going to get.

Changes

UNCLE VAI

We were crowded around the table in the far corner when she stormed into the patio.

I was just finishing up the last of my drink, getting ready to leave Jordan behind and walk home. We were trying to be friends again. He'd come along with me that Sunday afternoon and taken on a game with Colby, the youngest of the local pool sharks. All three of us had retired to the patio. Earl and Jude and Buster were already out there and we sandwiched in around them, bumping elbows and beers. And that's how we had passed a pleasant October evening, swapping jokes and tales as we talked for over two hours, as gay men can do, about our diets and our workouts and our habits, our conquests, our ex-lovers, and the cute guy at the next table.

Suddenly, there she was. She was strikingly beautiful, dark eyes, long black hair, mad as hell, fists clenched, lower lip trembling, looking for someone, looking, looking, glaring rudely into people's faces as her eyes adjusted to the darkness, and then suddenly stopping in front of Jordan.

Not that he doesn't always attract attention, as the good-looking of the earth tend to do. But the attention she focused on him was not appreciation. He barely had time to

Changes

give me an elbow jab, our time-honored signal, before she snatched up someone's unfinished drink on the next table and flung the contents into Jordan's face.

All of us exploded backward.

Guys went leaping. Stools went skidding. We were all much less concerned about actual physical danger than the possibility of staining our clothes.

"Hey, bitch, what the hell do you think you're doing?" barked Earl, our ex-con alpha male. He at once assumed authority even though he wasn't working that night. Messing with anyone in the bar was taken as a personal affront by our off-duty bartender, on the clock or not, and he was instantly standing beside Jordan and waiting for her to make one more move.

Jordan didn't notice. He was in another dimension. He acted like he didn't remember that any of the rest of us were still there, or notice the dark wetness splattered across his own chest. It was like all external sensory information had been interrupted. All he could see was her.

"Jessica!"

"I thought that looked like you," she said, as though it was the worst thing that could be said about anyone. "I saw this jerk running across the street in the middle of traffic, and he looked familiar." Jordan had a defiant habit of crossing the street wherever he felt like it, regardless of what that did to the nerves of caught off-guard drivers. He had gone out for a pack of cigarettes. If I knew Jordan, he had jaywalked coming and going. "And then I saw you run in here, and as soon as I saw what kind of place it was, I knew."

"Why are you in Seattle?"

"My mother lives here now." She swallowed, took a deep breath. "In a home."

"A home?" repeated Jordan.

She spoke so softly she seemed to be just mouthing the syllables. "A home for people who can't take care of themselves."

"I'm so sorry." Jordan sounded like he meant it.

"Because of you." She didn't say the words aggressively, but they seethed with hate. Jordan was genuinely taken aback. "Because of what you did to—to—"

"Me? It wasn't my fault."

"You pervert," she hissed. "You sick man, may God forgive you – because I never will!" She turned around and walked back to the door leading into the tavern, rudely pushing her way between two trim, broad-shouldered specimens posing in the doorway.

At first everyone in the patio was gripped in a moment of stunned shock. Then all of us at once struggled to regain our poise. Buster and Jude gave a few catcalls and obscenities. Colby and I re-positioned our stools and settled back down in our places again, all of us trying to avoid the wet spots and dismiss her aggressive unpleasantness with witty barbs and nervous laughter.

Changes

"What the hell did you do to make that chick so pissed off?" asked Buster, the stoned red-headed barista.

"It's a long story," said Jordan, nervously trying for the third time to light his cigarette. Buster took the lighter out of his hand, and did it for him.

The patio soon rumbled back into its various separate conversations. It wasn't the first time Changes had seen a little human drama. Jordan, however, didn't seem to be snapping out of it.

"Hey, are you all right? What was in that drink she threw on you? Is it going to stain?" It was so unlike Jordan to miss an opportunity to take off his shirt that I was truly worried about him.

He shook his head.

"Who in God's name was that?" I persisted.

"I really don't care to talk about it." His voice was thick with emotion.

I was too curious to be sensitive. "You've got to talk about it!"

"It's too personal." He then shocked us all by starting to cry. It was awful to watch. Jordan did not cry, and now I had to watch his shoulders twitch with a sadness he'd obviously kept bottled inside for years.

"Sorry, sorry, sorry."

"Believe me, you don't want to know."

"But I *do* want to know, Jordan," I said, and put my arm around him.

Changes

"Leave him alone," scolded Jude out of the shadows of the corner, his black face hidden inside the black hood of his sweatshirt.

"No, really," I persisted, but Earl interrupted me.

"Watch out, it's dripping off the table into your lap."

And it was. Earl grabbed Jordan's shoulder and pulled him away from the splattering trickle off the table edge. He knew right where to go for a wet rag. "Buster, isn't there another rag by the mop?"

The tall, lanky red-head returned with another rag, and the two big, strapping guys did their best to tidy up Jordan's damp lap. You'd think that would be enough to get anyone's attention, but my liquor-splattered friend hardly seemed to notice. His eyes were red-rimmed and wet, but it was like he wasn't inside his eyes anymore.

He'd gone back to the islands.

"I guess I've never mentioned my Uncle Vai?" said Jordan. "You'd know if I had." He looked straight at me. "You would have loved him. Your classic, cocky good-looking hunk. He was part Samoan, so he was big. Your cute bad-boy type. A little beard shadow. Angelic eyes. So handsome it made you ache just to look at him.

"I remember once watching my Dad stare at Uncle Vai. Dad's face got all tight and sad. 'That uncle of yours, he's too good-looking for his own good.'"

Changes

"Okay, okay," I said. "We get the point, Jordan." On the subject of good-looking guys, Jordan can drone on for hours unless stopped. "And what exactly does your handsome Uncle Vai have to do with this crazy woman throwing her drink in your face?"

"Jessica was there the night Uncle Vai was killed," he said quietly.

That did it. The mood changed. No one felt like laughing anymore. It was no longer a funny story. Looking from one face to another, we all thoroughly regretted asking to hear this story, which was going to be an unpleasant bummer. Any hope of recovering our light-hearted afternoon faded with the last light from the evening sky.

"He was killed?" I said the words softly, but it sounded like I'd shouted them. An uncomfortable chill had settled over the patio. "Jordan," I barked in irritation, "you've never mentioned this to me before."

"I don't talk about it," he snapped back. "Don't take everything so personally."

"And she – blames you for your uncle's death?" I asked incredulously.

His voice shook a little as he answered. "She's as guilty as I am."

"Guilty?" I repeated stupidly. I couldn't believe I was hearing right. "Hello? Excuse me, what did I miss? Guilty of what? Jordan, what exactly are you trying to say?"

Changes

His face got so solemn-looking I realized he wasn't joking and put my hand on his shoulder.

"Buddy, what is it? You've never even hinted at any of this before."

"Why would I want to?" said Jordan. "There are some things I would rather leave back in Hawaii."

"So you knew her when you were growing up?" said Jude out of the hooded shadows, trying to make sense out of what we'd seen.

"She was my first girlfriend," said Jordan. "We sang together in church choir when we were kids. Jessica and I were going to get married. I remember she cried for a week when my voice changed and I couldn't sing soprano anymore." He smiled wistfully. The smile was brief. "What caused the disaster in Uncle Vai's life wasn't Jessica." He shook his head grimly, remembering. "It was Jessica's mother.

"Carmen was something else. I can't describe her. She was the most beautiful woman I'd ever seen in my life. You think Jessica is beautiful, you should have seen her mother. All the men used to just stare at her."

"Your girlfriend here was a babe," said Earl. "Back when I was straight, I'd have gone for her."

"Compared to her mother," said Jordan, "Jessica was nothing. Carmen was the sexiest woman on the island. And she was untouchable. Everybody including Uncle Vai knew that Carmen was taken, that she had a secret boyfriend who gave her expensive presents and watched over her like a jealous guard dog. We couldn't figure out who he was, and we used to make jokes about this mysterious boyfriend. Everybody said he had a big penis and a big gun. Because of him, guys kept their hands and their eyes away from Carmen.

'Except for Uncle Vai.

"He didn't care. He was so good-looking, that guy, he was sure no one could resist him. And no one could, not even Carmen. They say he introduced himself to her boldly right in front of everyone in the supermarket. He got her phone number from his brother-in-law, Carmen's dentist. He started spending time with her, and then more time, and then he started spending the night, boldly, as though he could get away with it.

"Sometimes when I was playing with Jessica, I would see Uncle Vai coming or going. Once he came along with Mom when she took us kids to the beach. I saw him in a swimsuit. I'd never seen a body so wonderful. I followed him around shamelessly. I adored him. He used an aftershave called Island Fever. Once he put some on me. My mother yelled at him, 'Get that stuff off my kid!' But I ran screaming, I wouldn't let anyone catch me to wash it off.

"My mother always hated Carmen. Us kids never knew exactly why. Needless to say, Mom wasn't very happy to have me spending so much time with her enemy's daughter. But she encouraged the friendship." Jordan smiled sadly. "Jessica had one big plus in my mother's eyes. At least she wasn't a boy."

Changes

We all laughed, trying to shake off the tragic spell of the story.

"Your little Jessica has a lot of balls," said Earl. "To come in here and do such a shitty thing. But why does she blame you?"

"That's what I want to know," agreed Jude. "What does this affair between Carmen and Uncle Vai have to do with you?"

Jordan gave a deep sigh. "That part is harder to tell."

No one spoke, not daring to change the subject, waiting for him to go on. He looked intently at a place across the patio.

"You know how you're always reading about parents who beat their kids, and priests who touch altar boys, and teachers who fondle their little favorites. Adults are always accusing other adults of abusing kids. Everybody's always so sorry for kids who are poor innocent victims. Well, not all kids are so innocent." He tightened his lips, shook his head. "I was the worst, a total wild-ass hell-raiser. I'd do anything if it felt good. I had my first experience with a neighborhood boy when I was ten. I was cute and I knew it and I used it.

"And shortly after I turned thirteen, the devil got into my mind and made me set my goals on the impossible: on the most handsome man I knew. On that reckless hunk, my mother's bad-boy brother, Uncle Vai.

"He was my childhood god, everything a man should be. I couldn't get enough of him. I stuck to him shamelessly at family gatherings, followed him around like a heartsick

Changes

puppy. Night after night I dreamed of having those big arms of his around me. He was the center of my exploding new world of sex and bodies.

"One day I decided to make it happen. It was after dinner at a family picnic. I waited until Uncle Vai went into the bathroom, and then I went in, too.

"'Hey, can't you wait till I'm done?'

"'It's just me, Uncle Vai.'

"I stood behind him, waited until his penis was out and he was starting to pee. Then I asked him, 'Uncle Vai, what's masturbation?'

"He flinched. The arc of his stream wavered. I stepped a little to the side, so I could see his penis better.

"Uncle Vai chuckled softly. 'That's a question you should ask your Dad,' he said, re-directing his stream.

"I watched. 'Uncle Vai, can you show me how to masturbate?'

"That's all it took. I could see the change happening right before my very eyes. He looked away from me, and tried to hide it, but I'd seen it and he knew. 'Please, Uncle Vai, show me.' He shook his penis and put it back in his underwear, but he didn't zip up his pants.

"'I can't do that,' he said lamely.

"'Please. No one will know. Show me.'

"He agonized. In my memory, I can still see a drop of sweat rolling down the stubble of his cheek. I dared to bump one knuckle up against his underwear. He didn't stop me. I could feel his erection inside. So I took a deep breath and reached in."

Jordan's eyes were half-closed, remembering. We waited eagerly, hoping for lurid details. None came. "The next week I helped him unloading some furniture, and we parked the truck by the side of the road. The week after that, he helped my Dad with some plumbing, and I went with Uncle Vai to get some new pipes. We got the wrong pipes, and had to go back. Once he paid me to clean out his garage. Once he paid me to haul some rocks from the beach to his property. We always found time to be alone. I was totally under his spell. He ruled my world. I adored him. He taught me things. Whatever he said to do, I did."

The surrounding stillness of the patio made us realize how long Jordan had gone without speaking.

"And then?" I prompted.

"And then I made a mistake," said Jordan. "A bad mistake. One night when I had plans to go over to Jessica's house and sing together, there was a knock at the door. Uncle Vai was on the front porch. He'd had a few drinks. My parents weren't home. They'd gone to the soccer game. Everyone knew that. My Dad never missed one. Uncle Vai came inside and asked me if I wanted to do things together. I said yes. I forgot all about Jessica. I never called her to say I wasn't coming over that night to sing.

Changes

"She waited for me. She got boiling mad. Finally she came to the house. It was raining outside, so we didn't hear her come up to the door. She watched us through the window.

"And then Jessica ran home and told her mother."

We were the only ones left out in the Changes patio. The evening had turned into night without any of us noticing. We were all hunched forward over the table, listening intently.

"Carmen went nuts," said Jordan. "Ugly nuts. She was furious. She called her sister. Her sister called her friends. The story spread like wildfire. Maybe she wanted it to spread. Shaming my uncle for sexual play with a child was the perfect way to conceal her own guilty affair with him.

"No one took the news worse than my father. He came home that night and slammed the door behind him. He was utterly humiliated, red-faced with fury, as though the insult had been done to him. He slapped me. He knocked me around. He yelled at me a lot. I'd never seen him that angry. I don't remember a word he said. I was too terrified.

"He locked me in my bedroom, then got out his gun and loaded it.

"My mother was crying and shouting at the same time. 'Stop! What are you doing? Put that away. Please, no. Leave it for the police.'

When my father was like that, nothing could stop him. I shouted through the locked bedroom door. My little brother, Joseph, was crying in the next bedroom, just because he was so scared.

Changes

"It was raining that night, one of those awful summer rains that hit the islands every year. I heard the front door slam. I saw my father walk away through the downpour. He didn't even wear a jacket. I pounded on the door of my bedroom, I cried and cried, I shouted myself hoarse, I screamed, I couldn't talk the next day, but my mother wouldn't let me out.

"I didn't find out what happened that night until a year later, when Carmen's sister finally told me. She got the story from Jessica herself.

"Uncle Vai went to Carmen's that night, and at first she refused to let him in. Jessica heard them shouting for a long time, and then the shouting stopped. Carmen told her daughter that Uncle Vai would be spending the night.

"Hours later my father walked in the front door. He didn't knock. He had a key. Jessica hadn't gone to bed yet. She heard someone come into the house. She got out of bed, and looked. She saw him, drenched to the skin, go straight down the hall to her mother's bedroom. But her mother wasn't in the bedroom. They had finished their lovemaking, and Carmen was taking a shower. Uncle Vai was still in bed, passed out drunk.

"Jessica ran down the hall and looked into the bedroom just as my father covered Uncle Vai's face with a pillow. He fired his gun into the pillow twice. Carmen heard the gunshots in the bathroom, and screamed. My father fired the gun four more times. She rushed dripping down the hall, clutching a towel around her, just as my father was leaving the bedroom. He gave her back her key and told her to clean up the mess in her bed."

Jordan was shaking.

"But I didn't know that then. All I knew was that my father refused to look at me the next morning. He talked to me like I was human garbage, saying the few words he couldn't avoid saying to a spot somewhere just past my left ear. Then the phone call came, and my mother started screaming and crying. She hit my father, and everyone knew my father did it, but the police never came looking for him. No one dared to point a finger at him. He was too well-connected. He had done favors for powerful people."

We were hushed, stunned. What can anyone say to a story like that?

"What I don't understand," said Colby, "is how your father had a key to Carmen's house."

As soon as the words were spoken, we all knew the answer. I looked at Jordan. He nodded. "That's when we found out my father was her secret boyfriend."

No one knew what to say.

"It must have been awful for you," I said awkwardly.

Jordan shrugged. "When I heard that Uncle Vai had been killed, I thought the universe was going to end. I yelled until the neighbors could hear me. I kept screaming until my Dad slapped me silent. I cried myself to sleep. My little brother Joseph got so scared, he spent the night crying, too."

Changes

He shuddered. He closed his eyes. I drained the last of my beer. I started putting on my jacket, and was about to make my farewells when I realized he wasn't finished.

"Unfortunately that was only the beginning of the scariest night of my life." Then he told us the rest of the story.

I woke up suddenly. It was pitch black. I could feel right away that something was wrong. I could hear my father snoring down the hall. But I could also hear something else. I could hear footsteps, there in the house with us. Much too heavy for my mother or my brothers. Someone was in the hallway. Listen, it was not my imagination. You can believe this or not, but I'm not lying.

I got really, really scared. I was in a panic. I knocked on the wall between my room and my brother's room.

"Joseph?' I whispered. "Joseph, can you hear me?"

He didn't answer.

I whispered louder. "Joseph, somebody's in the house."

Joseph whispered something back, but I couldn't hear what he was saying because the door was swinging open. I was all scrunched up and whimpering, staring into the hall. There was someone out there. It was too dark to see much, but I could see a head, shoulders, an arm – it was a man. I was shaking with pure terror.

And then I smelled his aftershave. Island Fever.

It was him.

Changes

I was too scared to look at him, especially his face, but I could hear the floor creaking. He came into the bedroom and stopped at the foot of my bed. I started crying, but I didn't dare make a sound. My gut was twisting in fear because I knew why he was there. I was too scared to run, too scared to say no. He wanted me to do it again.

That's when my little brother Joseph came to the door. He took one look and started shrieking. He stood in the doorway, wetting his pants, his eyes bulging in fear.

"Joseph, what is it?" screamed my mother. She came rushing down the hall to my bedroom, afraid she'd find her kid executed the same way her brother had been killed the night before.

"It's Uncle Vai!" shouted Joseph. But there was no longer any trace in the bedroom of anything that could have been my uncle.

"Don't be stupid," said my father in his underwear, joining my mother in the doorway, his face an unreadable slab of stone. "You're lying, Joseph. Your uncle is dead."

"Uncle Vai!" wailed Joseph.

My father slapped him.

"Uncle Vai!" screamed Joseph, even louder.

My father slapped him again.

He would have slapped him again, if my mother hadn't stopped him. In my opinion, my little brother has never been the same since that night. That's when he began to hate my father. And for years afterward he always slept with his bed

Changes

surrounded by pillows, like some kind of feeble wall to keep away my dead uncle.

"Did you see who it was, Jordan?" snapped my mother, turning to me.

My father pushed her aside. "Jordan, talk sense to me. Who was it?" he demanded sternly. "Don't be a silly scaredy-cat like your brother. Tell me, what did you see?"

I was so freaked out I could hardly speak without my voice trembling. The stink of my little brother's urine made me hate him.

"I didn't see anything," I said.

"Don't lie!" Joseph wailed at me. "Uncle Vai was here! Tell him, Jordan!"

I looked my little brother in the eye. It was the worst thing I ever did to him. But I knew what my father needed me to say. "I didn't see a thing."

Joseph burst into tears. Dad took me into his arms. Sometimes you can only save yourself.

Changes

THE SPOILER

Anybody can knock over a drink. Anybody can knock over a stool. Knocking over both at the same time, however, takes a significant amount of impact.

Needless to say, it was involuntary. The last thing I want to do when I'm upset is attract attention. I want to retreat and hide my face and lick my wounds. I don't want everyone gawking at me. The clatter of my stool toppling over and the shattering crash of my drink attracted the complete attention of the bar that night. Not one person wasn't staring at me, as I stood there with my mouth hanging open, too stupid with my sudden realization to come up with anything smarter to say than, "You... you..."

Fortunately, not everyone was incoherent.

"We need a rag down here," called the guy sitting on the other side of me, who had jumped off his stool in time to dodge most of my drink. We needed more than the bartender's rag. The man staring at me, sputtering in shock and rage, had opened an old wound in my heart and stuck his fist in it.

This was no accidental meeting. His mysterious email had arrived yesterday morning out of the blue.

"Hey handsome, I've seen you at Changes lately," wrote a complete stranger who signed himself Lyle Brodsky.

Changes

"You don't remember me, but I remember you. Our paths crossed twenty years ago."

That got my attention. A chill crept over me as I continued to read.

"I got the guys at Changes to give me your email address off those photos you took at Halloween."

Oh. Well then, that's different. If the guys at Changes trust him, then he could even turn out to be some really great guy. This could be the beginning of a friendship.

"I know, I know, you don't have a clue who I am. Well, I know who you are. How could I forget the handsome, black-haired, energetic young guy with the awesome crotch – (how big are you, anyway?) – that I remember from Way Back When. You must have been free-balling in those days because there was always so much to watch bouncing around. You're still very cute, and now I can resume fantasizing about you!"

I'd stopped breathing without realizing it. I was completely disoriented. Not so much by the idea that I had an unknown admirer. I mean, we all do. That's not as disturbing as the idea of being watched unaware. Someone had a habit of watching my crotch? Where could I have known this guy?

When I wrote back asking him that, his reply was elusive and evasive.

"We've only had a professional acquaintance so far," he wrote. "And you don't even remember me. I'm going to be at Changes tomorrow night. Why don't we officially meet?"

Changes

My curiosity was too great to decline. The name Lyle Brodsky sounded vaguely familiar. But why?

The next day the city was slammed by a little classic Seattle weather. It came down in buckets. As usual, everyone acted like it was the first time we'd ever had to put up with such an outrage.

Then, without warning, just as I took one last look at myself in the full-length bathroom mirror and slid my arms into the sleeves of my winter jacket, resigned to be drenched, the rain mysteriously stopped. I stepped out onto my front porch into the drip-drip-drip of post-rain tree branches and leaf-stuffed gutters.

Folding up my umbrella and leaving it behind, I walked up the street sucking in shockingly clean, rain-filtered air. By some unconscionable stroke of luck, I proceeded up to Wallingford in a miraculous, moody intermission in the weather, the dark sky roiling with discontented clouds but no longer precipitating, the whole wet deluge pausing briefly, just long enough for me to reach my destination, like the parting of the Red Sea.

It started coming down again as I opened the black wooden door.

Friday nights at Changes are unpredictable affairs, sometimes crowded, sometimes deserted, with the highest lesbian attendance of the week due to a decade-long tradition of ladies gathering for the highly-economical Steak Night

Changes

Special. Tonight was no exception. A noisy crowd of beauties were gathered around the pool table. Having inhaled their weekly slab of red meat, they were making raw jokes and smacking each other's bottoms.

The little tavern was reasonably crowded, the tables all taken and most of the bar. I singled him out immediately, but not as fast as he spotted me. His gray eyes instantly had me nailed.

My secret admirer was maybe five years older than I am, a tall, lean man with unremarkable features, his cheeks flushed rosy, his neatly-shaped gray sideburns just slightly overgrown. A red flannel shirt was open at his tanned throat, the sleeves rolled halfway up his hairy forearms.

"It's so great to see you again," he said, warmly taking my hand in both of his and pumping it. "You've hardly changed. You're just as handsome. Now do you remember me?"

I had to admit I didn't.

"Well, thanks for walking up here tonight and taking a chance on me," he said, pumping my hand again. I would have told him that I had intended to come up to Changes anyway, except that his cell-phone suddenly interrupted us with a tinkly electronic version of Rossini's *William Tell*.

He glanced at the number and recognized it at once because he murmured, "Excuse me," and began mumbling into the little device. I couldn't hear what he said, but the tone of his voice was clearly meant to be reassuring. When he clicked it off, he glanced at me to see how much I'd overheard.

"My wife," he said.

I smiled, taking it as gay humor.

"No, I mean it," he affirmed. "A woman. A real one. I'm married." He read the look of bewilderment on my face. "I'm not out. This is my secret. I've got two grown sons and my wife doesn't know."

A revelation like that takes a moment to digest.

I tried to skirt around the topic and nodded toward the phone. "Is she all right? Has anything come up?"

"She's fine. She's visiting her mother. She thinks I'm at home. She just remembered some things she wants me to pick up at Food Giant. It's perfect. I only live a few blocks from here, and Food Giant is just across the street." He tucked the phone away. "Her mother lives in a condo downtown. Assisted living. My wife goes there three times a week. Which is when I come here."

Earl strolled past us at that moment on the other side of the counter, checking our drinks to see if we needed refills. "How about your old pal?" said Earl. "Are you still in touch with Bruce?" Earl was cleaning up the crumbs of somebody's chips. "How's he doing, anyway?"

Lyle's face turned a little grayer. "Bruce isn't doing so well," he said with a thickened voice. Earl stopped wiping down the counter. "Malignant – um, tumor, you know. Just got diagnosed." Swallowing clearly wasn't easy. No one was looking each other in the eye anymore. "Inoperable." That was just about as far as he could go at the moment, thanks to the break in his voice.

Earl mumbled his condolences and slipped away to get someone a vodka and tonic.

Lyle stared down at his drink, swirled the contents idly, and took several gulps. "Hard to imagine I could lose my best friend," he muttered. "What a life he's had. They live down in Palm Springs now."

"He has a partner?" I asked.

He nodded. "For sixteen years. Gorgeous, smart, fabulous guy. Only problem is, he won't sleep with Bruce. They're an ideal match in every way, but not that. No sex. Sixteen years of love and frustration for my poor friend, Bruce. And now a malignant tumor."

Maybe I just have an instinct for significant omissions. "So, tell me something. Is the problem that the guy won't sleep with *anyone*, or that the guy just won't sleep with Bruce?"

Lyle gave me a funny look. "Oh, he'll sleep with other guys, all right," he said with a blank expression. He finished off his drink without glancing at the liquid, his eyes drilling into mine as though determined to root out any information I might be hiding. "In fact, he slept with me."

My Long Island didn't quite make it to my lips.

"Too bad we got caught." The words were hardly loud enough for me to hear them.

Changes

"One day Bruce came home early. Took me almost a year to get his friendship back."

He went on, but I was no longer listening. As far as I was concerned, that was all I needed to hear. Sentence had been passed. It was a quick and easy judgment. This guy cheated on his wife. He cheated on his best friend. All I wanted to know now was where our paths had crossed before, and why he was coming back into my life, and I'd be heading out the door.

"So, you say we've had a professional acquaintance," I said, forcing the conversation back on target. "Meaning we've worked together?"

"I don't look even vaguely familiar?" he said. He forced his lips into a slightly bitter, unhappy smile. "You never noticed me, did you? You were pretty full of yourself back then. But I sure noticed you."

I ignored his comment. Young people are always full of themselves. "Well, I've only worked one place since I came back to Seattle from grad school," I said, "so you must have worked at the bookstore."

"Nope," he said.

"Well, then," I shrugged, "you must be mistaken. We've never worked together. It can't be me."

"Oh, it's you, all right," he said. "You just don't remember yet. Think about it. How about *before* grad school?"

At first I didn't know what he meant. Then it hit me. He was already smiling, waiting for the light to dawn.

Changes

"Right," he said. "*The Seattle Tribune*. You were the scholarship winner. You worked there during the summer as a copy boy." He hesitated just a moment before adding, "You used to hang out with Jasper Jamison."

Just the sound of his name was like a slap. I was overwhelmed with emotion. "Oh, my God. I haven't thought about Jasper in years." Jasper had been a copy boy the same summer I was, with one big difference: the Jamison family owned *The Seattle Tribune*, and Jasper was one of the two heirs. That reckless, mischievous, spoiled rich boy! I had adored that kid, all lanky six feet of him.

"Gorgeous, wasn't he?" said Lyle. Then he started to chuckle. He doubled over. I knew what he was thinking. I was thinking it, too. I could feel the laughter making my mouth twitch, until I couldn't hold it inside any longer.

"The Magnolia house?" I managed to say.

"Yes!" he cried.

We both cracked up laughing. Jasper had been a notorious space case, and one summer he ended up in the headlines of his family's own newspaper. He had been hired by some Magnolia people to house-sit their gorgeous new home on the bluff. Buster partied a little too heavily the night before, and forgot to turn off the sprinkler system when he left the next morning.

After three days, the bluff couldn't sustain the weight of the water-soaked ground.

Half the back yard slid into Elliott Bay.

Changes

We laughed a little more, the warm laughter of fond memories.

"God, I used to love that guy." That was an understatement. Given a chance to hobnob with legendary reporters, to hang out with the aggressive, hungry new bloods, I chose instead to pal around with the ne'er-do-well son of the newspaper's owner, a copy boy like myself. Of course, Jasper being a copy boy was just a stepping-stone in his career. He was learning about his father's empire from the ground up. I should have kept it professional. I should have known better. But soon I was too stupid with infatuation to help myself, adoring a rowdy rich boy who took off his shirt enough to capture my eternal attention.

Until our friendship abruptly ended.

"What ever happened to my old pal, Jasper?" I asked, trying to squelch the emotion rumbling up from my depths, trying to sound much more light-hearted than I was. Every life has its regrets, and the loss of Jasper's friendship had been a huge and guilty regret for me.

Lyle was paying a little too much attention to my face. "Well, it's not good news," he said. "The poor kid inherited the family curse. I forget the name. His father had it, too. Remember when the old man couldn't come to the office anymore? People who have it lose control of their motor skills, then speech. Finally they need total care. Jasper got so bad the family removed him from public view."

I felt like he'd slugged me in the stomach.

Changes

"What did they do with him?"

"They 'retired' him to a family estate in Idaho, I think. He passed away a few years ago. Very sad. You can be rich but you can't buy health."

His platitude rang hollowly. I'd forgotten my old pal was rich. All I could think about was that witty, wonderful guy, that unconscious, blossoming masculine beauty wasted by disease, crumpled and thrown away. If only I could have kept his friendship!

I was getting choked up. I had to stop thinking about Jasper and drag the conversation back where it belonged. "How about you? Where did you work?"

"I was the new guy on the copy desk."

I couldn't hide my sudden interest. "Really, the copy desk, huh?"

"Just on the other side of the room. Might as well have been the other side of the planet, for all you noticed. But I could see you from there. Lord, that crotch of yours could be seen from anywhere."

His comments annoyed me, but I let them pass. I was far more interested in his position on the newspaper. *The Seattle Tribune* copy desk had played a strangely pivotal role in my life. Finally I knew an insider who could solve for me an old and painful mystery.

"I'm trying to place you," I lied. "Now describe to me the copy desk, and who sat where. I want to see if I can remember which one you were."

Changes

I had a very good reason for wanting to know where he sat. Someone on the copy desk had watched me with Jasper and not approved. Someone on the copy desk told my high school journalism teacher that I was making a fool of myself chasing after the owner's son. Muriel Pall had summoned me back to the high school journalism classroom from which I'd graduated.

"Nicky-poo," said the dreaded bully, Muriel Pall. She could easily intimidate me, towering over me, all six feet one of her, hair yanked back in a furious little knot of a bun, glasses sliding down her nose, mouth hanging open to reveal blazing white teeth like prehistoric tusks. She backed me uncomfortably up against the blackboard with her sheer bulky mass, reeking of a big person's sweetish sweat, poking her finger into my chest, ruining my name with that degrading diminutive. "You've got to be a little more discreet, Nicky-poo. You've got everybody at the newspaper talking about you and Jasper."

How could I have let her call me that? I left my old classroom that day in a state of terror. How could I have behaved so carelessly? I was not going to throw away my entire career. I wasn't out of the closet yet. Was I really that obvious? Was I making a fool of myself?

Jasper tried to get me to explain what he'd done to offend me. How could I tell him how attractive he was? It would ruin everything. So I told him nothing. When he told me he was starting to drink again, I said nothing. When he told

Changes

me he was getting in fights, I said nothing. When he told me he got in a car accident, I said nothing. He was starting to stutter. One day he tried to tell me something, and couldn't. Then the summer was over, and I never saw him again.

Pretty sad, in retrospect.

Well, one of Lyle's pals on that copy desk was the reason it happened, and now was my chance to find out. One by one, he painstakingly described each one of the men who sat around the editor every morning marking copy. One by one, I saw their faces again. The skinny one with the cough. The corpulent bald one who sweated. The mousey guy with the wire-rimmed glasses who giggled at everything. And that pretty girl, Mary Ellen Something, who never said anything bad about anyone.

"Did someone on the desk take care of high school stuff?"

"That would have been Joe," he said confidently. "He did most of the education and outreach." I tried to picture Joe again. Bald, with glasses. "Or maybe Lou, if it was summertime." Lou, the old guy with the red nose. "Of course, it could have been any of us. I once spoke to a high school journalism class. Did it as a favor for a friend of mine. You may have heard of her. Muriel Pall."

All I had to hear was her name.

It was like sticking my finger in an electric socket. I stood up too suddenly. I knocked my stool over backward. I spilled my drink.

Changes

"Whoa, what's going on?" he cried, backing away from the dripping bar.

"You," I said dully.

"Excuse me?" he half-laughed at my complete disorientation.

"You're the one," I said. I never thought I would actually look him in the face. I was staring at the man who had broken something in my life. Lyle, married man, closeted gay, admirer of my crotch, liar and cheater, had told my high school teacher I was being too obviously gay at *The Seattle Tribune*.

Because of him, I stopped seeing Jasper.

Instead of a villain, however, all I could see was a man who'd lived his entire life in fear. His fear had kept him from being honest to his wife. His fear had prevented him from helping a gay boy out of the closet. His fear had poisoned an innocent, passionate friendship between two college kids.

I would have picked up my stool, but someone else took care of that for me. I had no further obligations. My night was over.

"Hey, where are you going?" I heard him call "I'd like to see you again."

I grabbed my winter jacket off the rack. He was still talking to me when I turned around and headed for the door. I don't think I said goodbye to my friends that night. I wasn't really thinking about Changes anymore, or about Lyle Brodsky, copy desk writer at *The Seattle Tribune*. When I

Changes

tugged open the door and strode out into the gray sheets of rain, all I could think about were Jasper's perfect, pale skin, his incredible jaw, that cleft chin, and that high-pitched, goofy laugh.

Walking home in the pouring rain, I imagined Jasper sprawling in the sun on that Magnolia patio, a beer in hand, headphones blasting, a perfect physical specimen lolling in the sun, while half the soggy, over-watered property behind him slid off the bluff into the bay.

Changes

BAD BOYS

When Jordan offers to give me a ride up to Changes, it's a sign he's in the mood to play pool. He won't come right out and say he wants to, or even that he's coming inside. He's just swinging by on his way home from the last doctor's office he's visited and giving me a ride. There's no way he can spend any time there. He has way too many pharmaceutical reports yet to file online before midnight, and laundry to do, and a mother to call.

But once he's driven close enough to the tavern to drop me off, he's usually too close to resist the call of the pool table. Not that he would actually say he was coming in. No, he simply parks the car instead of saying good night, and without explanation gets out, locks it, hands me his asthma inhaler to put in my pocket, and crosses the street with me toward the black, anonymous building front with the word CHANGES over the door.

He goes in first. He doesn't check to see who's there. He's looking down toward the end of the bar at the pool table, to see how big the crowd is, how many guys are waiting to play. Though everyone else inside is in casual dress and Jordan's still in his spiffy business suit, after his mafioso entrance it won't be long before he sheds the jacket, loosens

Changes

the collar, rolls up the sleeves, and tucks the floppy end of the tie out of the way, in between the buttons of his shirt.

When Jordan Perez played pool, he got serious.

Tonight he threw himself into the game with even more passion than usual. He'd been tense on the car ride over. He was just barely holding it together. Two days ago Eduardo said goodbye and boarded a plane back to Chile. The addicting summer passion came to a screeching, agonizing stop – a brutal interruption, and unless Eduardo got his visa renewed, the end. Meanwhile not only have his bills gone unpaid, his life is in chaos, and his business manager is questioning his hours and car use. His accounts have been neglected in a last reckless fling with the Chilean engineer who sidetracked Jordan's summer and inadvertently catapulted me into mine.

When Jordan turned around from the chalkboard waiting list for pool, the look on his face was not a happy one. "There are four guys ahead of me," he said. "Come on, let's play a game of darts. We've got time."

I'm not too bad at darts. I usually can't concentrate very well on strategy, but if Jordan just tells me which numbers to shoot for, I can come pretty close to hitting my target.

So that's what we were doing, me in a T-shirt and jeans, Jordan looking like a Wall Street shark, throwing darts together till his turn came to play pool. I was at the throw line, focused on the target, figuring out whether I'd shoot for the 18 or the 19, when a hand touched my shoulder and startled me, because it wasn't Jordan.

Changes

"Can I try that?" said this kid out of nowhere who was suddenly at my right elbow, standing up against me, his face inches from mine. At a glance, he didn't look old enough to be in there, like some little jailbait who could have played Puck in a high school production of *Midsummer Night's Dream*, a skinny colt of a kid, flat as a board, his blue T-shirt flopping around a scrappy body. But he looked good-humored, a cheerful lad who was maybe a drink or two into the evening and happy to be there.

"Sure, give it a shot."

He took one of my darts in his hand, took my place at the throw line, and threw, missing his number by a couple of inches.

I threw next, and missed as well. I threw again, and did even worse. The last dart, to my humiliation, didn't even stick in the dartboard, but boinked off onto the floor at the kid's feet. He handed it back to me.

"What happened?" he grinned.

I grinned right back at him. "Guess I was distracted."

To my surprise, he poked me in the belly with his finger and winked.

He told me his name was Jamie and offered me his hand. I could tell from his accent that he wasn't a Northwest native. He was cocky and funny and looked like he didn't weigh much more than a hundred pounds. He had a gash of a mouth in a tiny head, a little pug nose and big, buggy eyes.

"Let's see if you can get one to stick," he said.

Changes

"I'm trying."

"I can tell."

He laughed a lot. His eyes sparkled. He bumped up against me, grinning.

I'm always caught off-guard when anyone who meets Jordan and me chooses to flirt with me. Jordan is the hot little people magnet. I'm the tongue-tied watcher. But this kid didn't flirt with Jordan, even when Jordan won his first game and the two of them ended up playing pool together. He was competing with Jordan, but I was the one he kept looking in the eye from across the table. I was the one he stopped beside to talk.

Then without explanation he walked away from me and sat down on the other side of the pool table, where he was unexpectedly joined by a big, bald guy whose head was covered with tattoos.

Suddenly the evening veered off in an entirely different direction.

Jamie no longer appeared to see me or remember who I was. Clearly this guy had something to do with the change. I hadn't noticed him before but he immediately monopolized all of the kid's attention. He sat down beside him and had his hands all over him. Jamie didn't appear to object. The big guy was loud and annoying. Jamie seemed to adore him.

The guy had to be his boyfriend. He certainly wasn't a looker. His head was covered with swirling blue lines. He had a Genghis Khan mustache, several punctures, several steel rings. I don't remember where they all were, eyebrow, lip, nose, ear, the usual places. He wore a black T-Shirt that was uncomfortably snug on his considerable overspill of body. The words on the front of the T-shirt were probably funny if you took the time to read them, but they were in small type and there were far too many of them, all bending and curving over the ample proportions of his gut.

Clearly this guy's presence explained Jamie's sudden chill. Who is this guy who has such an effect? He must have gone out to get money from a cash machine or buy cigarettes or get stoned. Or maybe the two of them had arranged to meet there. Now the guy wanted all of Jamie's attention, and Jamie was willing to give it.

Meanwhile, Jordan was challenging Jamie to a rematch. The boyfriend called out to him too loudly, "I'm betting on you, Jamie. Fifty dollars says that you win. If you win, you get the fifty. I mean it." After letting us all know he had fifty dollars to throw away, he said, "He's my Ken doll, that boy. I call him Ken. For two years I called him Ken. I never did learn his real name."

I was growing to dislike this guy more with every passing minute. And listening to him wasn't optional, because there was no escaping his booming voice.

"I made you what you are today," he called out to Jamie, as the kid was lining up a difficult pool shot. "Don't fail me." Jamie smiled at the guy insulting him, and pretended he didn't see me.

Changes

From aggressive interest to chilly indifference, his attitude change baffled me. Had he been scolded for flirting? That didn't seem likely, since he seemed to be flirting with several guys on the other side of the room. I watched him back up laughing into a man's lap while making a difficult pool shot, and Jamie made the most of it. The boyfriend seemed to enjoy the joke and fun of it all.

I alone had been erased from the picture.

Well, you can't let weird guys throw you, or you might just as well go home right now. The bad boys are out there, they're unpredictable, they can hurt you, and you have to let it roll off you and move on. Which is what I was doing, enjoying the pool game, chatting with Jordan in between shots, when the kid crossed the floor straight toward me until he was bumping up against me.

"I don't want you to go away with the wrong idea," he said. "I'm not a shit. I like you, too. You and I really connect – but I'm straight."

"You're what?" I groaned. "I can't believe it. If there's one straight guy in a crowd of fifty gay men, somehow we'll find each other. But how about your boyfriend?"

"Who, Jeffrey? He's not my boyfriend. He's the guy who saved my life."

"What?"

"Come over here." He drew me away from the crowd, put his hand on the back of my neck, and leaned closer,

Changes

talking directly into my ear above the loud, pulsing music of the video above us.

"I'm from South Dakota. You may ask, why did I come to Seattle? I'll tell you why. I had to get out of there fast. Don't ask me, so I don't have to lie, but let's just say it had something to do with what is technically called auto theft. I thought Los Angeles first, but I hated it there. Now Seattle, this is a city I could live in. Long as I can keep out of trouble."

He laughed at the very thought, a kind of down-home, country-boy chuckle. "You can't imagine how much trouble I can be. I was one helluva bad boy when I came to this town. Just turned seventeen, spent most of my money on bus fare, hitched the rest of the way, running away from everybody, had to be tough because I look like I'm about twelve.

"Let me tell you, gays tried to hit on me. Always do. Well, I fucking hated gays. They scared the shit out of me. Hope you won't turn against me when I tell you this, but I was a gay basher. Yeah, I don't look the type, do I? I kicked the crap out of some older guys and took their wallets. Believe me, I could be a real shit. Well, that's how I lived. That's how I survived. I robbed a couple old queers. And I was all set to do it again, getting ready to rob this guy walking all by himself in the park, this fat guy with tattoos on his bald head.

"Well, instead of coming on to me, he offers me some food. So I think, great, I'll get into his house and rob the sucker, too, and so I go with him. Well, he cooks for me, he treats me like a king. When I tell him I feel grubby, he lets me

Changes

clean up in the bathroom. While I'm shitting and in the shower, he washes my fucking clothes.

"He doesn't try to touch me. I would have killed him, I was so scared. But no. And he gives me his bed and he sleeps on the fucking sofa.

"What am I supposed to do? Rob him? Beat the fucker up? No. I'm stuck. I had been sleeping in the basement of a church with two other runaways, and now I've got a place to live. This guy buys me clothes. He helps me get my first job. And when I turned twenty-one back in May, he took me out for drinks, one in a straight bar, one in a gay bar. You know what? I had a better time in the gay bar. I always do."

The pool game was over. The place was thinning out. Jamie wanted to go to Neighbors, where gay kids mingled with straight in a thundering all-night disco. Jordan wanted to go somewhere he could keep playing pool. I pulled on my sweatshirt, tugging it down over my head, and when my head poked out of the hood, there was Jamie, wrapping his arms around me in a hug.

"Hope I see you here again soon," I manage to say before Jeffrey blocks him from view.

Jordan drove me home, playing his current favorite song so loud that talking was impossible. I sat back and let the night lights wash over me through the windshield. I understood why the music was so loud when he pulled up to the curb in front of my place and turned off the engine. He slumped forward over the steering-wheel with a sob.

Changes

"I hate feeling like this." He sniffled, wiping his wet face on his arm, wretched enough to allow himself a rare moment of frank self-assessment. "He had no money. His visa was expired. He had to get back to Chile. What could I do? No one else could help him. I bought his ticket for him."

He beat his forehead against the steering wheel.

"I know, I know, stupid. He used everyone. That's how he survived. And you know what? I don't care. I'm still crazy about him. I had a saint for a boyfriend and I gave him up for a South American trickster, but you know what? Eduardo gave me a taste of the best sex I've ever had in my life. I never knew it could be like that." He groaned. "What if he doesn't come back? I hate him! I hate him!"

I don't like watching anyone cry.

I know, I know, Jordan can be pretty damned selfish. He deserves whatever he gets for all the lies and betrayals and cheating he's done. I suppose we all do. I wrap my arm around his shoulder, and he wipes his messy nose on my shirt.

Those bad boys, once they hurt you, it's like a tattoo. It's too late to change your mind. It stings like hell, and you wear the pain for the rest of your life.

Changes

NOT-SO-GREAT EXPECTATIONS

There's a car heading straight toward you with your name carved into its grill. You can see it coming but it's still far away. You tell yourself not to worry. You're convinced you're safe. There's plenty of time for it to turn aside. There's plenty of time for it to brake. After all, you're on the sidewalk. You're out of harm's way.

I'm walking to Changes expecting a fun night, looking good, casual, confident, butch. So what if it's raining? I've got an umbrella.

It's a downpour, all right, but hell, it's Seattle. I'm cheerful, and feeling healthy and alive. What harm can a few drops of water do? It filters the air. Take a deep breath – yes! I'm wearing that short green T-shirt that looks so good on me, the faded jeans that fit me the best, and the few raindrops that sneak under my umbrella only create a windswept look.

I have no idea that tonight will be my last night at Changes. I think it's just one more night, the usual, a couple hours, one drink, and I'll be heading home. I haven't a clue that my visits to this little Wallingford bar are about to come to an end.

If anything's coming to an end tonight, it's smoking cigarettes in Seattle bars. This is the last legal night.

Changes

Maybe I'm thinking about that, maybe not, maybe I'm just enjoying the rhythm of my stride and the night breeze and an illogical optimism, holding up an umbrella against the rainstorm.

I've crossed the freeway bridge and I'm most of the way there, just passing Dick's Drive-In, the hugely popular, old-time Seattle fast food icon. The sidewalk is crumbling on the corner. The road dips and sinks.

There's a huge puddle.

I must have looked too happy, too filled with high expectations, smiling under my umbrella in the rain. I must have looked like some simple-minded, optimistic clown who thinks life is a musical.

What I looked like was a walking target.

A car swerved up close to the curb. That was the last thing I saw.

Then all I saw was a wall of water…

The sound of water slapping down on the pavement made me realize what had happened. I hear laughter and a toot-tooting car horn. I'm drenched. I'm stunned to be so completely, thoroughly wet. I'm in shock. It was like a tidal wave coming right at me. Look at me. Tell me this didn't happen. I'm trying to go backward in time, to somehow avoid this moment, to erase it, to start over, but I'm stuck, sopping wet in the present. I'm only three blocks from Changes. This is how I'll be arriving for my evening social hour – dripping, I mean soaked to the skin.

Changes

I don't remember walking the rest of the way to the bar. I'm in denial. I'm thinking if I just ignore it, I'll soon be dry. Long before getting there, my attitude has bottomed out, my spirits have collapsed. My expectations, which were limited but buoyant, have plunged.

Not that they were that high, to start with. My goal had always been somewhat cynical. I wasn't looking for an Adonis with personality. All I wanted was a reasonably attractive, reasonably sane guy who was interested in more than a one-night stand. Was shooting for a second date with the same guy asking for too much in the gay world? Was that expecting unreasonable odds from life?

It hadn't happened in month after month of walking up to this little bar. How many years would I have to invest in darts and pool, karaoke and Long Island iced teas? I was fooling myself. It wasn't going to happen. Not there, not anywhere.

Which leaves me where I am now, standing on the sidewalk in front of the black door into Changes, dripping wet, without enough conviction to reach out and grab the door handle. It's a cold winter night, and I'm already regretting the walk up here. What do I think I'm going to find in this little tavern? I'm afraid to admit I'm wasting my time. In my heart, I don't believe I'll ever find anyone in a gay bar.

It certainly isn't going to happen when I arrive there sopping. But I've come too far now to go home.

Changes

Just reach out for the door handle, open the door into this friendly little bar, and forget about your loneliness and wetness for an hour or two. Go ahead, reach out for it. This is going to be a fun night. And remember what you've got in your coat pocket!

That afternoon I'd seen an ad in *The Stranger* and come up with a great idea. Right after getting off work I bee-lined over to the Woolly Mammoth shoe shop on the Ave to pick up two free passes for an advance screening Monday night of the movie I most wanted to see this fall – the new Ang Lee film, *Brokeback Mountain*.

The ultimate gay date movie.

Armed with my free passes, prepared to ask the right guy out on the date of the year, I'm here to find him, whoever he might turn out to be. And there will be plenty of guys to choose from tonight, that's for sure. The place will be packed, in a last haze of legal cigarette smoke, steamy warm against the downpour outside.

It's a historic night in Seattle bar history, the end of cigarette smoking in public places. We've been hearing all kinds of rumors about how this particular little bar is going to celebrate the end of an era, including a special beacon on the last night that will show all the smoke in the air. The new non-smoking ordinance goes into effect tomorrow. Too bad I'm soaked, but that's how it goes. I wouldn't miss this particular night for anything.

Changes

I push open the creaking black door and walk into that loud, dimly-lit den of stools and glass mugs and fluorescent beer logos, of pool balls clicking and bursts of male laughter, a separate reality with a pulsing house beat – the bar, the television screens, the framed male nudes.

Changes is jumping. More and more guys are bumping and elbowing their way inside. The more crowded it gets, the more cigarette smoke thickens the air, blurring the bar into a soft-focus fog. Buster, the pierced barista, is leaning back against the wall on a stool with a huge cigar in his mouth. When I greet him, he doubles over coughing.

"I didn't know you smoked cigars."

"I don't," he wheezes. "I just thought I'd try it tonight. I'm not doing so well." He slides off his stool and gives me a hug. "Come back in an hour, I'm bartending later." He disappears into the smoke, which has never been this thick and never will be again.

In spite of the festive crowd all around him doing their best to smoke and drink and talk and laugh at the same time, Jude looked like he wasn't having a very good night. He was slumped over at the bar, his head in his hands, his little black dreadlocks all askew. His grubby white T-shirt looked like he'd worn it driving his truck today, which meant he hadn't gone home from work yet, which meant he had a reason for not going home. Three little shot glasses were lined up in front of him, empty.

Changes

I stood to order my drink beside him. He didn't look up. I grabbed his shoulder. "Hey, buddy, how's it going?"

When he saw it was me, his black eyes brightened. He hugged me a little too long. "Don't mind me," he said. "I'm fine. It's just trouble at home, the usual. He says he's not going to move out."

Jude's roommate, Daniel, was a source of endless grief. According to Viking, the guy was insanely in love with Jude and that's why he wouldn't move out. Of course, that didn't explain his not paying rent. According to Jude, the guy had needed a place to crash for a month and then didn't leave, just cooked and washed and cleaned. Jude has repeatedly given him his walking papers. Daniel refuses to walk.

"Long Island?" said Shawn.

With a sweep of his hand across the bar, our charming young bartender for the evening walked up and deftly removed the three empty shot glasses. When I didn't correct him, he began pouring from one bottle after another, adding an extra dollop of something, and saying, as he usually did, "Oops! Better watch out. This is going to be strong." He turned to Jude. "Anything else, boys?"

Having a twentysomething call me a boy cracked me up, and I smiled at him. That was all it took – one good look in the face – for me to realize that, unlike his usual cheer, Shawn was radiating a palpable sadness.

"No, thanks," said Jude. "We're doing fine, sweetheart."

Changes

Shawn was the youngest of Changes' three bartenders, a goofy, willowy kid with a quick wit and a quick smile who was growing into a charming, solid young man before our very eyes. His hair was short-cropped and changed color periodically, his youthful frame was filling out. He was sassy and good-humored.

An old timer beside me leaned over his drink and said, "Back when Shawn did afternoons, we all came here every day just to enjoy that kid's company. He knew all our names. He knew what everyone drank. Had a smile and a kind word for everyone. He could have charged admission."

Shawn was a special favorite on karaoke nights. He was known for standing outside Changes with his arms hanging limply and jumping up and down beforehand to loosen up, to release some of his nerves. Then he would stride into the bar, grip the tall mike with one hand like a dance partner, and lunge and sway with it as he sang.

Easy to see what was different about him tonight. Shawn wasn't smiling. He looked like all his inner organs had been surgically removed, and he was trying to have a good attitude about it. Something was missing, and Shawn was putting on a brave face to hide the ache. I could feel it, even when his back was turned. I turned to Jude, but Jude had only been waiting for me to notice.

"That boy is hurting," he said.

"What do you mean?"

Changes

"You know what hurting is," said Jude, rolling his eyes at me. "Take a look at him. What makes a boy look like that? He's hurting for someone. How blind *are* you? Can't you see when somebody's in love?"

I felt like a complete dolt, and took another look at Shawn. Admittedly he didn't look good, like he'd been giving blood at a donor bank and been left bleeding too long. His hands were pouring and scooping and squirting and shaking and stirring, but his heart wasn't in it.

"Doesn't look like love to me," I said. Being soaking wet can put you in a cynical mood. "Looks more like the flu."

"But that's exactly it!" Jude bopped me on the head. "Love is like any other virus. Your resistance is down. Suddenly you can't think straight. You get chills. You break into sweats. You lose weight. You spend all your time in bed. Just like a virus, once you catch it, there's nothing you can do but wait it out. It has to run its course. Then you recover. Or you don't."

Toodling musical notes burst out of Jude's cell phone. He popped it open and answered it immediately, then looked up at me and mouthed the word, "Daniel," so that I knew he'd be in an emotional tizzy within moments. I left him clutching the phone to his ear and gripping his dreadlocks with the other hand, as though trying to pull them out.

A short little pool shark named Jojo was beating one gay guy after another, and out-butching them into the bargain. I hoisted myself up onto the metal shelf over the coolers to

Changes

watch her and one contender after the next stalk the solids and stripes, letting the night happen to me. That's where I was sitting, finishing up my Long Island, when Colby came in, the youngest of the Changes pool regulars.

Colby has a unique look summed up in a single word – angles. He's got a square jaw on a square head, and long, skinny arms and legs on a long, skinny torso. When he plays pool with a long, straight cue, it's all a ballet of geometric positions, of leg-arm-cue coordinates measuring angles with angles. In the karaoke world he's carved himself a niche as the one Country Western singer at Changes. The biggest grin you'll ever see on his face is when he's belting out "Red-Necked Woman."

Colby was a car rental salesman by day, not the fast-talking stereotype but the kind who worked out plans with insurance companies. On his long commutes back and forth to Renton he practiced Country Western tunes, singing in the car as he waited in freeway jams or bridge traffic. Nights were his to break loose, which usually meant coming to Changes, playing pool, checking out the guys, taking home the ones he wanted. He looked barely twenty-one though he was approaching thirty, a guy of few words but friendly, few smiles but warm ones, a television sports fanatic, an addicted pool hound.

"How's your love life?" he asks, racking the balls.

I make an appropriate sound of dismissal. "Not much to talk about. How's yours?"

Changes

He winked and made his shot. "Complicated," he said. "Tell me. Does it ever get easy?"

I shook my head. "Nope. If it was easy, everyone would do it."

"Do you ever feel like, no matter what you do, you hurt people?" he said, quite earnestly. "You can try not to hurt people all you want, but sooner or later someone gets hurt."

"It's your shot," said Jojo. The meaty little lesbian was patiently waiting to beat him.

He aimed his cue, his mouth a grim line of determination. The eight ball rolled right up to the edge of the hole and stopped. Jojo quickly set about ridding the table of the rest of the stripes.

"I mean, you think you know people," said Colby, "and then you go home with them and they're totally different. What are you supposed to do?"

"You mean like the he-man soccer player who changes into a lace nightgown?"

He laughed. "Exactly. I mean, do you expect to find a teddy bear on the bed of a hot guy you go home with? Sort of a turn-off, huh? So, big deal, I laughed when I saw it. I made a comment. Is that so terrible? Dating is the shits. I prefer pool any day. I'm going to put my name up on the board, if you don't mind. Next time I'm gonna beat her ass."

"Teach her how to play, Colby."

My straw made a slurping sound at the bottom of the ice cubes. I turned around to set down my glass and noticed

Changes

Jude putting on his jacket, taking down his backpack from the coat rack. I left Colby to his pool game, leaving a wet smear behind me on the counter, and went down the length of the bar to say good night.

"Okay, now let me think about this," said Jude. "I don't want to get on the wrong bus."

"Come on, I'll go with you."

As Jude and I were walking out, we heard something crash in the little kitchen. From where we were standing, it was only a couple steps around the end of the bar into the kitchen doorway.

Calling it a kitchen is an exaggeration. It's got ranges and convection ovens and microwaves and grills, chopping board and refrigerator all piled into a space the size of an airplane bathroom. Shards of a broken plate and French fries were splattered all over the floor.

Shawn stood over them. His shoulders were shaking. His hands were over his face, and he was making wet, choking noises with his nose and mouth.

I immediately backed out, feeling like I was intruding, but Jude stepped across the mess and took the young bartender in his arms. No customers asked for drinks during the time they were back there, so it couldn't have been long. I stood in the doorway and said, "He's fine," to a couple inquiries. Then Shawn was wiping his eyes, putting on his professional face, and stepping out of the little kitchen toward the bar.

Changes

As Shawn passed me, eyes bright with pain and determination, he said to no one in particular, to the God who is always listening, "Fucking teddy bear, making such a fucking big deal out of it."

And he was gone, taking orders.

At first I didn't understand why Jude was shaking me. I was too busy staring at Shawn behind the bar and Colby beyond him at the pool table.

"Come on, walk me to the bus stop," said Jude. "Make sure I get on the right bus. And don't let me forget my backpack at the bus stop, either. Last time I had to take the bus all the way back to the bus stop to get it. And you gotta tell the bus driver to wake me up on Broadway. Tell him not to let me sleep past my stop again. He let me sleep all the way to downtown. I'm too tired to walk back up that hill."

I wasn't sure he was going to make it through the doorway. The minute the door opened, the night breeze stung our cheeks and slapped us to attention. Jude lurched. I grabbed his arm and steadied him. We left Shawn to serve drinks and Colby to shoot pool, and set off for the bus stop.

I've often wondered what might have happened if I hadn't gone back to Changes that night. I'd seen what love did to Jude. I'd seen what love did to Shawn. Partners could be a living hell. Yet I still went back into Changes to look and wait and hope just a little bit longer. If I'd given up and gone home, as I intended to do. I might have

Changes

happily continued going to Changes for years to come. As so often is the case, my fate hinged on an "Oh, so what?" kind of decision, one of those silly moments where you think that your choices don't matter. Another hour at Changes – how can that make any difference?

Making sure that Jude was securely bundled into the right bus, with my cold wet clothes clinging to me, I impulsively decide the night isn't over yet and open the black door a second time.

But not all the puffing and laughing and attractive men in Seattle can lift my spirits. I scold myself for not leaving when it was sensible. Instead I'm alone in a crowded gay bar, a very wet man, a very lonely man, and I have two movie passes in my pocket.

I'm completely disoriented and demoralized when tall, lean Buster startles me by reaching across the bar from the service side and grabbing the tip of my nipple through my shirt, wringing it mercilessly. "Why the gloomy look, butterball? How about a smile?"

I writhe in pain. "Ow, ow, ow."

"You're looking a bit damp," says Buster. He finally lets go. He always seems vaguely amused by pain, as though he's left such minor distractions behind. "You need a drink. What'll it be? No, don't tell me."

Buster has taken over for Shawn, and is bartending alone for the first time tonight. His lanky body is attractively sheathed in a white thermal shirt that fits him snug as a

Changes

condom. He's a little insecure, but his nervous puppy look makes you perfectly willing to wait for anything.

"You are the wettest man in this bar tonight" he says, scratching his eyebrow ring. "What the hell happened to you?"

"I got soaked out there."

He checks me out, laughing. "So I noticed."

"It was a wall of water." He looks at me blankly. "Puddle. Car." I mime the rest, with sound effects.

He grins. He's a doll. "Oh." He throws me the bar rag. "You look like you were baptized."

"Thanks." I manage a half-smile. There's not much a rag can do, and I throw it back at him. "How're the kittens?"

Buster's cat recently surprised them with a litter. Buster and his boyfriend couldn't bear to give the kittens away. Now their house was overrun by five tireless young males gleefully ripping the furniture to shreds.

"Oh, they've taken over, but they're letting us continue to live there."

He sells me a Long Island for $5, less than any other bartender would charge. Then he buys the entire house a round of drinks. Buster would like nothing better than to be a regular bartender at Changes.

Everyone's in high spirits here, except me. I slosh back half of my second Long Island. That ought to do the job. I shrug out of my wet coat, hang it up on the rack, and slide up onto my old familiar metal bench above the coolers to watch Colby play. I'm on auto-pilot, more tired than I thought. My

Changes

mind is starting to blink out. Pool balls are only so interesting. I forget who has solids and who has stripes.

I'm really not looking, but I gradually can't help but notice a reasonably cute guy sitting at the end of the bar who fills his maroon sweater nicely, and who seems to be aware of my presence. He's got a boyish face, a mousy little blond mustache and a bit of a tummy. To my delight, he slides down off his bar stool and comes over to challenge Cody to a game. In the process, he introduces himself as Tyler, and includes me in the introduction.

He seems interested in me. He sits next to me on the pool bench, and we begin chatting in between his shots. He dares to sit closer, and then a little closer. We're clearly courting each other, a touch to the shoulder, a touch to the thigh. He's got just one year left before becoming a nurse, and does intern work at Overlake and University Hospitals. He broke up recently with his lover of four years. You can tell he's still having a hard time over it.

Tyler and I hit it off. We're clearly focused on each other, and not pretending otherwise. We start adding little intimacies to the conversation, all the little touches and pokes, rubs and bumps of playful physicality. Our hands linger. The questions get more personal. The answers get a little more honest, more vulnerable.

He admits to descending into crystal meth addiction, but proudly tells me he managed to pull out after six months, before it destroyed everything he was shooting for.

Changes

"My lover wasn't so lucky."

We eventually move over to sit on bar stools and almost get ready to play darts together, when he asks, "How far away from here do you live?"

I say, "Oh, about two miles. Shall I invite you over?"

He responds, "That's up to you."

"Well, I can at least give you my card." I fumble in my wallet, pull out one that's not too worn. But when I give it to him, he seems to consider accepting it, then presses it back into my hand.

"Actually, I'd rather have a date."

"A date?"

I lead him over to the rack where my coat is hanging, guide his hand into my coat pocket, and close his fingers around the two passes to *Brokeback Mountain*.

I don't know it yet, but that's how easy it is to come to a sharp turning-point in your life. Tyler is exactly the kind of guy I came to Changes to find. He's about to come home with me, and we're going to have an unforgettable first date. We'll begin seeing each other intensely and exclusively. For a few months he'll be the most attentive lover I've had in decades. He'll whisper compliments in my ear, give me life-shaking blowjobs, wash my dishes, fold my clothes and make my bed. He'll attack my face with kisses, until I can't pull away and don't know where I am. He'll let me fuck him till my knees turn to rubber. He'll lead me, step by step, act by act, deeper into sexual obsession than I've ever gone with anyone.

Changes

I am about to realize how much of my life I spend every day hunting for the right guy to love. Suddenly I won't be hunting anymore. All my little habits are about to change. I've walked through a wall of water, and on the other side I'm going to learn something about love.

We kiss. He's holding the movie passes and right there in the bar we kiss. A long kiss. He cuts off my air. I almost lose consciousness. Now he'll feel how soaked I am.

"Notice anything strange about me?"

He looks at me with a confused smile. "No. Why?"

"I'm sopping wet." When he doesn't look appropriately impressed, I go on. "I'm drenched. I'm soaked to the skin. I'm one hundred percent wet."

"Are you?" He looks amused, and kisses me again. "I didn't notice."

We go back to kissing, and why not? The search is over. I've found what I was looking for. This is it. He's the essence of what was missing in my life, the reason I've been patiently going back to that little bar night after night for months. I've finally found him, an attractive equal, a partner, a playmate, a real gay relationship.

I've stumbled into the beginning of a head-spinning passion, one breathtaking date after another, a whirlwind romance, an electrifying sex life. It's an overturning of my stale old habits by a maddeningly attractive man suddenly sharing my life. To continue going to the little bar any more seems pointless. Why ask for trouble?

Changes

I stop going to Changes.

Tyler and I will date exclusively and passionately for six months.

Then one night he'll bring home a powdery white surprise in a folded-up square of paper and we'll have the best sex of our lives. After that, all stories are the same. Once you've tasted the forbidden fruit, there's no going back to paradise.

I escaped, that's the only difference.

I'm about to finally get what I've come to Changes looking for, and it will be a brutal lesson in having your wish granted. In six months when Tyler leaves me only the luck of the angels will keep me from following him in his plunge to the chemical depths. I'm about to learn how messy and frustrating and complicated loving another human being can be. By then my landlords will have reclaimed my floor of the house, and I'll have moved to a new home that's no longer walking distance away from a little gay bar.

*